Stone Heart

Stone & Flame Book 1

Mallory Glass

SLOTH & ENVY

PRESS

Sloth & Envy Press LLC

Cover art by JV Arts https://www.justventurearts.com/

Chapter image art: Camsyn Clair @beingcam.bsky.social(feather)

Sloth & Envy Press – Visit our website https://slothandenvy.com

Sloth & Envy Press logo courtesy of Fran McKinney

Author's illustrated headshot by Christine Ridgway at SkidarStudios.com

ISBN: 979-8-9923631-0-4   e-Book ISBN: 979-8-9923631-1-1

I would dedicate this first book to my mom, but she would never say the word cock out loud, so I'm not sure she would have appreciated having a spicy monster romance dedicated to her. I love you and miss you anyway. This book is not for you.

Notes

This book contains material that is not suitable for readers under eighteen. The sex scenes are explicit and very much open door. You've been warned!

Contents

Lauren

I stand beside my rented Fiat, using one hand to shade my eyes from the sun as I stare up at Kinloch Manor. It's an amazingly well-preserved medieval three-level tower. The whole structure, tower and attached manor house, could fit inside the courtyard of Edinburgh Castle. I'll be working here for the next few weeks on a special restoration project. It's the first solo venture for my new business, and happy anticipation wars with anxiety inside me. That the job brings me deep into the Scottish Highlands adds an extra dimension of pleasure to this journey.

My hungry gaze takes in the granite guardians of Gothic Revival architecture adorning the façade. I take my time examining the rough exterior of the stone manor, ignoring the beauty of the neatly landscaped grounds.

Most people don't know or care about the subtle difference between grotesques and gargoyles. Kinloch Manor has an intriguing variety of grotesques, and although they make little architectural or historical sense here, I find them delightful. I can't wait to get my hands on them.

"Ms. Townsend, welcome."

Startled, the squeak that slips out of me resembles a noise like a rubber dog toy being squeezed by a Rottweiler. I spin around to find an older, well-dressed man standing to my left. His craggy face is etched with deep lines around his muddy brown eyes and no lie, the man wears a kilt. I try not to stare at his knobby knees and hope a stiff breeze won't give me a reason to learn what a Scotsman really wears underneath the garb.

"Lauren, please. Nice—"

"I'm Lord McCardle." He eyes my extended hand and his lips twist at one corner. "If you'll follow me, Ms. Townsend, I'll escort you to your room in the upper tower."

"Upper tower? I thought I was staying in the gatehouse."

"A change of plans."

He sets off for the manor, and my wheeled bag thumping over the cobblestones echoes my annoyance at the change in plans.

"Ms. Townsend?"

Lord McCardle's crushed gravel voice calls to me from the top step and I blink, breaking the spell that had mesmerized and locked me into place with one foot poised on the bottom step of the front porch.

"Is something wrong?"

My cheeks flame in response to getting caught staring up at the figure high over the south entrance.

"It's fine, I just...I had the strangest feeling of being watched." My lips clamp shut and I shake my head in bemusement, joining him inside the foyer.

"You'll be on the upper floor."

Dammit.

An enormous tapestry hanging on the wall across from the staircase captures my gaze. The hair on the back of my neck stands up. For the second time since I arrived, I freeze in place, losing touch with my surroundings.

A fierce snake, its fat coils wrapped around a group of three swordsmen, squeezes the life from them judging by their expressions. The enormous head looms over a second group of frightened people, some fleeing, others cringing or kneeling. The snake's solitary eye gleams red.

"The family crest," McCardle says, startling me yet again.

He gestures to a smaller scene woven in the tapestry. Another snake wraps around the thick branch of a tree, tongue extended to scent the air. Its fangs are bared and it lunges toward a faceless form, ready to swallow the small figure whole.

"Ahhh," I say, and curse silently at my inability to form a lucid response. "I've never seen a crest quite like that." My voice is a mouse's squeak. I still can't take my eyes off the snake in the crest.

"The tapestry is centuries old," he says, mistaking my awe for something other than sick fascination.

"Do you even have snakes in Scotland? It seems an unusual choice for a—"

"Perhaps we could discuss this later," he says, cutting me off. Again. *Rude.*

I shrug it off and continue up the stone staircase with him.

I'm in good physical shape at thirty, but I struggle to catch my breath after hauling the suitcase up three (*and a half!*) flights of stairs. If I had known about the change ahead of time, I would have packed lighter.

"The work crews will arrive first thing in the morning to set up the scaffolding and movable platforms under your supervision."

"And the bosun's chair?"

"And the harness, yes." The corner of McCardle's mouth twitches.

No doubt *Lord* McCardle finds the idea of a woman hanging off the side of his precious manor highly distasteful. I hide a smirk behind a polite cough.

McCardle leads me down a long dimly lit hallway, passing through multiple sets of doors.

"Your room is in the highest turret, near the roof access stairwell. The doors we passed through will be locked, so you'll need to enter and exit the manor via the staircase outside your room."

Trailing behind him, I roll my eyes.

"Here we are." He opens a door at the end of the hallway and gestures for me to enter. The entryway offers no light and my steps falter. He flicks a light switch on the wall and I step into the room.

The small room is barely more than a closet, but tidy. Sunlight streams through two small windows and dust motes dance in the beams. The electric sconces on the wall provide a dim, yellow glow. Between the windows a small writing desk and chair wait for an occupant. A milk glass lamp sits on a rickety nightstand. It rests next to a twin bed. Those two pieces alone take up one side of the room.

Five bucks says the mattress is lumpy. My inner voice blows a raspberry.

"The WC is at the end of the hallway."

How many luxury bedrooms are there below us, and here I am shoved into an attic space, and now the toilet isn't even ensuite. And that bed...

I long for the promised gatehouse.

I need this job.

"You may of course make use of the kitchen, which is to the left at the bottom of the staircase. The exit to the outdoors will be to your right." He shrugs. "Cook goes to town once a week. If you need anything, let her know. We are minimally staffed, but fresh linens will be provided, just no housekeeping service." He gestures to the nightstand. "There are lanterns and candles in the event the power goes out. It happens sometimes during storms."

"Is there a Wi-Fi password?"

"Wi-Fi?" One regal eyebrow lifts. "I thought you understood we're quite isolated here. You can, of course, use the café in the village, where they have a somewhat stable connection."

"Mobile service?"

The eyebrow lifts again, and he doesn't need to answer.

"Uh, yeah, thanks." My left eyelid twitches. *I need this job. I need this job.* I repeat this internal mantra until I can smile my appreciation at the man.

The stairs to the rooftop access where I'll be staging the majority of my work are no more than five quick steps outside the bedroom door.

"Would you like to inspect the roof now?"

"Ah. Um, I'll have a look after I unpack. If you don't mind."

McCardle seems eager enough to part company without a rooftop tour.

"I'll leave you to it." He nods and shuts the door, leaving me standing alone in the middle of the room, a princess locked in a tower with no way out.

Excitement makes falling asleep difficult that night, but after a restless hour, the sandman finds me.

In my dream, I'm standing on the rooftop terrace, enjoying the nighttime view. The crescent moon shines, and the stars twinkle overhead. Even though I can't see the nearby pond that I know is out there, the distant frog chorus gives away its location. Torches blaze at the four corners of the seating area, casting eerie shadows.

I sit on the stone bench and take a deep breath, even though I'm aware on some level that you can't smell in dreams. Nonetheless, my nose detects a hint of jasmine in the air.

A shadow flickers in the corner of my eye, and I stiffen in alarm. A cool presence settles at my left elbow, and I discover I'm unable to turn my head.

"An uninvited human enters my domain." The accented voice is deep and smooth, like the surface of polished marble.

I shiver and tell myself it's the cool night air. A chill I shouldn't be able to feel in a dream.

"A dream." The voice sounds skeptical. "Believe as you will if it is easier."

Even without seeing him, I'm aware of what manner of creature has settled beside me. I recall the pictures in my contract packet.

He's the largest of the manor's grotesques, a lion-like creature with stubby wings sprouting from his back—wings that would never support flight—and a tail wrapped around his right flank.

The pictures showed a short mane, a halo of human hair surrounding a face more man-like than bestial. The front paws are less leonine, giving an impression of oversized human hands.

His second most striking feature, the one I spent so much time studying in the photos, is how his head lifts to the skies, face locked into an open-mouthed roar of defiance.

The *most* striking thing about him is the artist's decision to carve him with a rampant erection.

On second thought, maybe the look frozen into stone isn't a roar of defiance at all. Maybe...it's ecstasy.

"Once you know why I'm here, you might be a little more welcoming," I say, lifting a hand to grope for his hard shoulder. My hands are calloused from working with stone, and unlike other men, he doesn't complain about the roughness when my touch settles on him. "I'm here to restore you to your former glory, after all. You and the others." Fingertips trace tiny fissures and pits, scars inflicted by time and weather.

"My *former* glory?" Venomous pride drips from his words.

His growling disdain brings a smile to my face and I'm glad now that I'm not looking at him. "Well, you are looking a little weather-beaten, my stony friend." *God, this is such a weird dream.*

I shift my eyes to the left, an attempt to gauge his reaction. There's only deep shadow. The stone warms beneath my hand, and the heat spreads up my arms, taking away my chill.

"You don't sound very Scottish." I expected my dream to have a more authentic flair, really.

He stiffens and growls. "I am not *Scottish*, wench!"

I muffle laughter at his outraged tone, and pat his shoulder to placate him. The tense muscle relaxes.

"Tell me more of your purpose," he says.

Never one to pass up a chance to discuss stonework, I detail my plans for the restoration of the six grotesques that decorate the manor. Altogether there are seven, but the lone figure on the north side has been damaged beyond repair. McCardle proposed that if he's pleased with the restoration work, he'll contract me to carve the replacement figure. For now, I'm to remove the remnants of the old piece and prepare the area to receive the new one.

The last part of that masterpiece left after being struck by lightning and worn away by the elements is a woman's vulva, and oddly enough, her feet. They are poised as if she had lain on her back and drawn her legs against her body, feet to the ground, exposing the very center of her being for all to see. It's not surprising. Entire cathedrals in some countries are covered with phallus-wielding chimeras and wanton gargoyle women.

The stony shoulder feels more flesh than granite where I've rested my hand.

"Ah, poor Selene," he says, and the sorrow in his voice brings tears to my eyes. "While she was only ever a passing fancy, she did not deserve what became of us. Perhaps now, with the destruction of her prison, her soul flies free." He sighs. "And so it may be that she is the lucky one, after all."

He stretches, and his muscles bunch under my hand. I catch a glimpse of his near-human paws flexing.

His lips touch my ear and I flinch in shock.

"You may call me Adriel." His tongue laps my earlobe, rasping and dry. This time, my tremor can't be blamed on the cool spring night. "And return to me with the rise of the moon on the morrow."

The stone tongue flicks behind my jaw, tracing the tender spot below my ear. My lungs burn from holding my breath. Trapped in his hybrid form, I wait to see if Adriel will act as lion or man. Will he thrust his tongue down my throat or tear it out with his teeth instead? My fingers tighten their grip on his short mane.

He fades away. The torches blink out, extinguished as one, and I'm left with a sliver of the moon and distant stars for light.

With the departure of Adriel, the night surrounding me grows empty, and that emptiness claws its way into my belly. My dream slips away into the ether and deep sleep claims me.

Adriel

S unrise locks me into position on the south wall, and my nighttime ramblings come to an end. I can still monitor that intriguing
woman from here, even if I can't interact until nightfall.

Nights at Kinloch belong to me, though it's been some time since
I chose to wander.

And what has brought her into our dark prison? Restoration, she
says. Curiosity stirs in me for the first time in...well, who can keep track
of time's passage anymore. Not I.

This modern era amazes me. A lone woman, here to revitalize our
stony exteriors. And perhaps our stony hearts.

And yet, who is responsible for bringing her here? She may be one
of *his*, Cardle's, sent here to tease me out of the shadows with her
alluring laugh and tart tongue.

Cardle, my eternal enemy. It's been some time since he's visited his
estate. When present, he does his best to ignore me, as most of his
family has tried to do for generations. Except for the ones I drove mad.
Oops.

The staff prove too wary to approach. Cook, an old witch like her mother before her, engraved protection runes over many of the bedroom doors so that I cannot visit in the night. My magic, once a match for that of Cardle, has worn ever-so-slowly away, much like my granite prison.

But now comes Lauren, arriving at the new moon and on a wave of interesting auguries. Just last week three stars fell from the heavens in a stunning display. The letter A appeared in a spider's web in the corner of my stone ledge. I do not know what other message it had for me, as a bird came and made a meal of the spider. Unfortunate, that. Most believe a bird shitting on your head a good sign, but I know from a wealth of experience it's nothing special. I'm sure I saw a rabbit hop backward not a week ago. Change rides the air, I sense it writhing in the currents.

When she touched me, the world shook and I could almost believe myself a man again.

Lauren

Nothing wants to go right today. The workmen arrived late and didn't get everything set up before it was time for them to make the long drive back to the city. It means booking another day for them to return and finish, so I left that task to McCardle. He'll get a better response. I know how to pick my battles, and it's best to keep arguments with people responsible for installing your safety lines to a minimum.

Always know whose hands hold your safety lines. The thought intrudes and rattles around in my head.

My last job, before I left to start my own business, was with a masonry restoration company owned by my ex-boyfriend. I was the lone woman on the work crew, and they let me know my presence was tolerated only because the owner wanted me there. My ex, the man who made me team lead and paid me less than the rookie employees he hired. The man who wouldn't protect me from my co-workers' sly resentment.

Worse, the work was straightforward and involved no real artistry. No real heart.

After my dream last night, my fingers itch to work on the lion (*Adriel*, my mind whispers). I stick to the original work plan and lower myself down the north facing wall using the small moveable platform. There's time to start on the remains of poor Selene in the last hour or so of lingering daylight.

"I don't know if that's really your name." I pat one of her remaining scaled feet. Her grotesque form had been a dragon-human hybrid, with clawed hands and exposed fangs. "It's pretty, though, so that's what I'll call you."

I continue chatting with Selene, reviving an old habit. I use the mallet and chisel to knock away pieces of her left foot. "I'm starting to feel like I'm conducting a weird pelvic exam," I say, tossing a stone toe into the bucket.

This morning over tea, I reviewed pictures of Selene before her destruction by the elements. I focused on her half-closed eyes and parted lips. It's obvious that the original artist captured lust rather than horror.

"I'm just sorry I couldn't save you, Selene." Regret flows from my fingertips into the granite remains. Another chunk of stone lands in the metal bucket with a soft *bong!* and a droplet of water splashes onto the rock.

Oh hell, why am I crying? I swipe the back of my hand across my cheeks, annoyed.

"I'll see you tomorrow, my orgasmic friend." A chuckle bubbles up, and I sniffle before pulling myself together. Time to call it quits for today.

"You cried for Selene today," Adriel says, taking his place at my side.

"Really? This dream again?" Everything about the rooftop remains the same as last night. "I'm starting to think I suffer from a lack of imagination if this is the best I can do."

"Is it?" His hot breath on my ear prickles my skin. "The best you can do?" His mouth closes on my neck. Despite the gentle touch, I'm reminded of a predator's jaws ready to snap shut on its prey and drag it into the brush to consume.

"Uhhh." My head tilts away, exposing more of my neck to him. I forgot what I wanted to say. *Something something, clever remark inserted here.* God, he's so warm, the granite heated by the day's sun.

When I try to turn my head toward him, his teeth press into my skin.

"Why can't I look at you?" My pulse throbs under the tip of his tongue as it traces its way to my jawline.

"It's not time yet."

"What?" My hands come up, but instead of pushing him away, I stroke the wild mane of hair. The stiffness of the stone wavers under my touch, and my fingers dig into wiry locks.

"Close your eyes." His lips trace the shell of my ear. He pants like he's run for miles, raising the hairs on the nape of my neck.

Oh, what the hell, it's a dream. It's *my* dream. I'm going to enjoy it while I can. After I squeeze my eyes closed, he presses me back against the bench.

"So delicate." The low murmur of his voice reminds me of a stream burbling over rocks. Solid stone paws, no, *hands*, grasp my knees. I huff out surprise at the strength in the fingers. He could crush my bones with a light squeeze.

"I won't hurt you," he says.

Does he sense my fear the way a wild predator would?

The smooth hands run over the tops of my thighs, leaving a trail of flames in their wake. His fingers tug at the edges of the fabric he encounters. "Interesting," he says.

Dammit. I can't even have lingerie on in my own sex dream? The faded t-shirt and floral print boyshorts I wore to bed prove a thin shield between me and my stone beast.

His fingertips travel beneath the hem of the shorts, and my eyes start to flutter open. He growls low in warning. I exhale a shaky breath and scrunch my eyelids closed.

Warm flesh replaces the heaviness of stone, and feather a touch over my outer folds. A grumble of pleasure from Adriel and a flush rises from my neck to my cheeks. There's no hiding the evidence of my arousal from his questing fingers.

"These are in my way," he says. With one hard pull, he shoves my shorts down to my ankles and exposes me to the cool night air.

My stiff nipples rub against the fabric of my t-shirt. Clothing that once felt soft now irritates like sandpaper.

Adriel says something in a language I don't recognize, but it sounds like he's swearing. His hands return to my thighs and shove them apart. Something between a growl and a purr rolls from his lips, lips that have found the inside of my left knee. The kiss he places there burns the nerves beneath my skin.

"Oh."

I'm surprised to find the tiny spoken word belongs to me. It's the only word I manage to squeak out before Adriel drags his rough tongue up the inside of my thigh. The rocky flesh smooths out, softens, and leaves a trail of saliva to mark its wake.

"Oh." Blood roars in my ears in time with the pounding of my heart.

He inhales, and this time he does growl. I squirm and he spreads one hand on my hip bone. The other lands on my sternum, pinning me to the bench.

"What are you doing?" My hands grasp his wrists, the skin beneath my fingers stiff.

"Tasting," he says.

If his hands hadn't been holding me steady, I might have flown off the bench when his mouth brushed my sex in a delicate kiss.

"Eyes closed." He warns me as if he knows my struggle to obey the command. His tongue darts out and laps from the bottom to the top of my slit.

My eyes flutter beneath closed lids and I dig my nails into his wrists. For once, the stone doesn't yield to flesh. Only his hands and hot mouth provide any human warmth.

"Oh my god," I whisper to the night.

"Pray to any deity you desire." Amusement warms his voice. "In my time, we worshipped many gods and goddesses." Against my thigh, I feel his lips curl into a smile. "But no goddess ever turned up to lie beneath me until you, my blossom."

Oh. Wow.

"B-blossom?"

His tongue slips between my folds, plunging deep inside of me. Adriel's moans mix with mine, echoing around the little rooftop terrace, bouncing off the stone and carrying up into the open sky. I strain against his hands, longing to rock my body to the rhythm of his mouth, begging for more without words. The bench scrapes my skin, and his grip on me firms.

I dig the fingers of one hand into his hair, and he lifts his head.

"Full of sweet nectar, and ready to bloom for me."

Heat travels straight to my core and spreads like wildfire. *Best. God-damn. Dream. Ever.*

Adriel doesn't wait for a response. He lowers his head, and returns to his task with renewed vigor. My hand fists in his locks, and my panting is harsh and loud in my ears. He's fucking me with his lips, his teeth and his tongue, licking and sucking my clit until I'm whimpering with desperate need.

"Adriel." I rasp out his name, not certain he can hear me over the ravenous sounds he makes feasting on my soaked pussy. I'm on the edge, waves of pleasure lapping at my feet, ready to pull me under. "I need...I need..." What do I need? I'm babbling, incoherent through the haze of sensation. I tug at his hair, but he ignores my demand.

"*Please*, Adriel." My thighs clench around his face and his rumble of laughter throbs in the center of my being. The wave catches me and I cry out, my walls pulsing around his tongue, that clever organ working to wring every drop from me.

I'm boneless beneath his hands, spent. He drags his mouth away, kissing my damp inner thigh, working up the crease of my leg, tickling his tongue in the hollow at my pelvic bone. My chest heaves, my breathing loud against the stillness of the night. I loosen my grip on his hair.

The hand at my hip moves, sliding the edge of my t-shirt up and over my belly button, where his tongue pauses to play. He shifts, and a heavy weight brushes against my thighs.

"No!" I flail, panicking, certain he'll try and thrust that massive stone erection into my body and rip me apart.

He's saying something, but my racing heartbeat drowns it out. My eyelids fly open, and he flinches back. The loss of his warm hand brings an instant chill to my skin.

My brain can't process what my eyes see. He flickers like an old film running on a bad projector. A mane of black hair, a human face, and in an instant he's a fanged beast again, snarling in the torchlight. His body twists and a human hand emerges, and then morphs back to stone.

He spits words in that ancient language, and I'm falling...falling...

The muffled roar of a lion pierces the night. I jerk awake, flailing. And then I *am* falling, crashing right out of the narrow bed onto the stone floor.

"Uhmph." I lie still, and assess myself for broken bones. Nope, all good. I shove to my feet, groaning. *Of all the whacked out ways to ruin a perfectly good sex dream.*

My boyshorts and thighs are damp, and I cover my face with my hands, though there's no one to see my blush. Oh god (*any deity you desire,* Adriel's voice whispers), please don't tell me I had an orgasm in my sleep.

I so did.

I fumble for the bedside lamp and flick it on, blinking in the harsh light. With a sigh, I perch on the edge of the bed and rest my elbows on my knees, catching my breath and working hard not to sink back into the memory of the dream.

Unlike most of my dreams, this one, this twisted tale of a granite sex god who gives great oral, hasn't faded away like a wisp of smoke upon waking. I'm torn between reveling in it, and hiding my head under the blankets.

I catch sight of a dark mark on my thigh. *Adriel marked me.*

Sure, yeah, okay. I snort uneasy laughter. It's probably a bruise from bumping into something and I didn't notice earlier. Stonework isn't juggling cotton balls, after all.

My lower back burns and I probe raw skin with my fingertips.

"What?"

Ah. I must have scraped it when I fell out of bed.

Or when you freaked out that Adriel's massive cock touched you, and you ruined the be—

Yeah, yeah, best sex dream ever, I hear you. Shut up!

"And now I'm arguing with myself in the middle of the night." I throw my hands into the air. "No. No, no, no."

Blanket tucked around me, I press my warm face into my cool pillow and count to ten, taking slow, even breaths. Flopping onto my other side, I take ten more breaths.

My clit throbs.

"Shut. Up," I tell it. "You had your fun tonight, and you are done."

Sleep comes, but it's far from restful. I dream without remembering.

Adriel

T hree nights without Lauren, waiting for my long-dormant magic to rebuild itself after she shattered my spell. She visits the rooftop, but she resists crossing into my domain. And so we are separated by the Veil, until my power can draw her to me again.

None of the others trapped by Selene's mate can work even a hint of magic, dooming me to wander nighttide alone these centuries past. The staff grew used to me decades ago and do their best to ignore my presence. Cardle pretends I don't exist, and I first thought he brought Lauren to preserve his crimes. Now, I sense other things stir in this closed universe of ours.

My chance at freedom may have arrived in the form of my blossom, my nocturnal goddess. Recalling her responsiveness, a low growl rumbles my chest. Centuries of nights alone, but after two short intervals in her company, I hunger for more. I fed my power on the core of her, marveling at the way her touch drew my humanity from the stone.

And before this transformation could bring me to my *true* 'former glory', she slipped from my grasp.

She believed I would have hurt her. Frustration ripples along my form, and I howl rage into the night. The stone beneath my feet trembles. In the room below, Lauren tosses and turns in her sleep, dreamless and alone.

How well I know that restless state and the empty night.

I've always had too much of a poet's heart for my own good.

Lauren

I stand near the fountain in the center of Kinloch's courtyard and stare up at the leonine presence jutting from the wall of the second story. My eyes burn from nights of restless sleep, the kind where I can't get any refreshing rest. Between that and the physical exhaustion of cleansing Selene's presence from the north wall, I'm a wreck.

"I'm sorry!" I shout up to Adriel, hoping my voice carries to his perch. "Come back, okay?"

"Ms. Townsend?"

I whirl to find Creepy McCardle behind me. My cheeks heat in answer to being caught shouting at the guardian of Kinloch Manor.

How does this guy keep sneaking up on me? He's not even supposed to be here.

"Ah, hello. I was just, uh, apologizing to Ad-" I struggle to come up with an excuse that doesn't sound insane. "The uh, lion...about the delay in getting to work on him." *God, that sounded dirty.*

McCardle's face clouds with suspicion, and his glare bounces between my face and Adriel. He tears his gaze away from the great beast and clears his throat.

"Is everything, ah, going well with the project?"

"Oh yeah, great. Really fantastic. Right on schedule." Mostly. "Have you got the workmen booked to return for the next set up?"

We talk shop for a while, and McCardle can't resist a few more covert glances skyward. Some of his questions probe into areas outside the work. Am I satisfied with my accommodations? Am I scared to sleep in the upper tower without anyone around? He takes more interest in me, and the work, than he's shown before. Communicating with McCardle always had a touch of mystery, but I'd assumed it was due to him being a Lord of some kind and me a part of the working class.

He ends the discussion with an abrupt nod when I'm mid-sentence and scuttles off to his car. He throws one more fleeting look at Adriel before he jumps in the car and drives off.

Interesting.

"There goes a guy who knows how to kill a party!" I yell up at Adriel, not caring if the staff see me carrying on this one-sided conversation. Adriel, ever-vigilant guardian of the main entrance, stays stubbornly silent. *Prick.*

The third time my chisel slips while I'm working on the west wall's devil dog, I call it an early day and go in search of Cook.

Cook is one tight-lipped lady. I can't get anything out of her about McCardle or the manor, not even her scone recipe. She's not sharing anything, providing one word answers to any question I ask, or a murmured, "Ask Lord Mac."

Annoyed by the reticent 'Lord Mac' and his even more reticent Cook, I slip away to the rooftop to watch the sunset over the distant hills. Brilliant pinks and yellows paint the horizon, and I daydream about dragging the thin mattress off the bed and up to the roof so I can sleep under the stars. Maybe I'll drive into town over the weekend and look for a camping mat.

The idea of watching the stars emerge in the night sky enamors me. I concede to the need for comfort and dash to my room to grab my pillow and duvet.

By the time the moon rises above the edge of the roof, my body complains about lying on the stone for too long.

My eyes drift closed.

"Lauren."

I jolt awake, stiff and chilled under a blanket of countless stars above. Adriel sits in shadow, nothing more than a dark shape near the door. Relief tinged with anger sweeps through me.

"Where have you been?"

"Waiting to return to you. Close your eyes, Lauren."

So he'll know how irritated I am with him for taking so long to visit me again, I heave a huge sigh. *Are you blaming a stone lion for not showing up in your dreams?*

Well, yeah.

I close my eyes.

He mutters a garbled word, and the stone roof melts into a soft bed of moss beneath me.

"Oh. Nice. You're full of neat tricks."

"Yes," he says, tone dry. "Neat tricks."

Cool stone settles at my side. I roll over and loop an arm around his rigid front leg, stroking the smooth rock. It warms under my hand and Adriel purrs with pleasure.

"How do you do that? You're a stone grotesque."

"Such manners. I am no mere grotesque."

"Is it because it's a dream?"

"It's not a dream." His human hand envelops mine, and places it on his granite face. "Touch me, Lauren. Bring me forth."

"But I can't look?"

"Not now. Not yet. I don't have enough power to hold my form in the face of your, oh, let us call it disbelief." Muscles flex beneath my hand.

The smell of wet pavement after a rain shower permeates the air, and I inhale my favorite scent deep into my lungs.

I rise to my knees, eyes still closed, and run my hands over his twisted face until it relaxes and reforms under my touch. My fingers tingle, and the sensation flows up my arms and into my shoulders. It's the second best feeling I've had since I arrived at Kinloch.

"How did you come by your magic?" he asks.

I laugh at the idea. "I don't have any magic."

"Your accent is unusual."

"It's not that unusual. Well, maybe in Scotland it is." I lean into him. "I'm from Joplin, Missouri. You know, I'm American."

"America." The word rolls off his tongue like he's tasting something new. "Ah. Yes. It is on the map on the library wall. America."

Adriel catches one of my hands and kisses each fingertip. His other hand mirrors my actions and he strokes my face with a light touch. His thumb traces my bottom lip and I give it a delicate lick. The mineral taste of salt lingers on my tongue.

Adriel's breath catches, and he wraps a hand around the back of my neck. His lips brush across mine—once, twice...

The growl starts deep in his rigid chest.

The third time his lips meet mine, he nibbles gently and pulls back. My lips try to follow, but I'm held in place by that firm hand on my neck.

"Stop teasing me," I say.

He chuckles and proceeds to do just that with light kisses that never linger too long. Adriel isn't content with tasting my lips. He slides his mouth along my jaw until he can nibble my earlobe. Whispered words I don't understand caress my ear and shivers run through my body. He traces his tongue over the pulse in my neck to my collarbone.

The urge to open my eyes is strong, but this dreamscape of mine runs on rules. I don't want to ruin it like last time. Too many nights passed before I could summon this beautiful world again.

"I want to see you," he says, his voice low and gravelly in my ear.

"Yeah, well, I know the feeling."

"Don't sulk, my blossom. Stand and remove your garments. Let me see you."

"It's dark."

Adriel sighs and pulls out of my grasp. Annoyance pricks me and I open my eyes. He's retreated to the far corner, where one of the rounded turrets meets the square roof.

Light blooms and I throw up a hand against the sudden glare. Four torches appear on the roof, one at each of the cardinal points, like the night he brought me to a toe-curling climax.

Adriel's nothing more than a black shape nested into a gray corner.

"Remove your garments, lie back, and close your eyes."

"Why are you bossing me around in *my* dream?"

"It is not a dream," he says, impatience evident in his tone. "Do as I say, and I will offer proof."

"How?"

"You first."

Am I really going to strip naked and stand on the roof of Kinloch Manor for the amusement of my dream's grotesque?

Oh my god, I think I am.

Laughing up at the sky, I tug my shirt off and toss it aside. I'm bare beneath it. The torches provide enough heat to drive back the chill of night, but the skin around my nipples puckers, tingling and sending a shiver down to the base of my spine.

I shove my shorts and panties down in one smooth move and kick them to the side.

"Now you." I raise a brow, taunting Adriel.

A rumble emerges from the corner, but it doesn't sound angry. My nipples tighten in response, and I bite my bottom lip. Heat blooms between my legs. If I touch myself, my fingers will come away damp. My lips curve in a half-smile even as I continue to chew my lower lip.

"I need you to feed me, Lauren."

It crosses my mind that I stand less of a chance than a gazelle on the tundra. They at least have four legs to run and the ability to take great leaps. Any leaps here and I may plunge to my death on the flagstones below.

That flash of fear morphs into a memory of Adriel spreading my thighs and eating me out until I screamed his name. My cheeks heat up at the memory of his tongue and I choke back a whimper.

"Down," he says, laughter marring his voice.

Damn him for always seeming to know my thoughts.

"What will I get?"

"Besides untold pleasure?"

"Yes. Besides untold pleasure, you insufferable egomaniacal lion."

"I'll tell you a story," he says, as if he's always known my love of lore and how to tempt me with such a promise.

Of course he knows, he's your weird dream. Duh.

"After you feed me," the smug voice says.

Grumbling out loud masks the pounding of my heartbeat as I lower myself to the mossy ground. The slickness between my legs reminds me this is feigned reluctance.

I close my eyes and sigh into the open sky above me. My body tenses, and I wiggle my toes to dispel nervous energy.

A presence at my right arm and then Adriel's lips hover over mine. *I wish I could see your face!* I fight back the urge to sneak a peek and suck my bottom lip between my teeth. He uses one fingertip to tug my lip free and taps it.

Warm, strong hands grip my shoulders. They're flesh, not stone. He rubs small circles into my collarbone with firm pressure. Not heavy enough to concern me, and not so light that I'm not treated as fragile. The right touch.

The hands travel at a slow pace, exploring at leisure, leaving my shoulders and finding the tops of my breasts. His breath hitches and the knowledge that I'm not alone in my responsive lust fills me with unexpected warmth.

"Your heart is beating so fast." The low murmur causes my toes to curl.

"And yours?"

His hands hesitate. I reach out, and locate his arm. My hand rides over his bicep, to his shoulder, and stutters to a halt on his stony chest.

"Never mind that," he says. "It's been still so long I might die of fright if it began to move in my chest again."

"That's sad." I whisper the words, but I'm not sure if he hears. I pull my hand back to my side. I'm uncertain what I should do with them since my touch seems to have cooled and the stone stays unchanged.

Adriel's palms scrape over my nipples. They harden and I bite back a moan. His large hands cup my breasts. The strength in his fingers lights up my nervous system and I shift restlessly against his touch.

"It's been so long," Adriel says, but I don't think he's talking to me.

He rolls my nipples between his fingers, and my spine arches. The growl is back in his throat, a low vibration in the night air that brushes my skin and seeps into me through his fingertips.

Torture. Sweet, delicious torture where there's only pleasure, and that pleasure dances on the borderline of pain.

He continues teasing me with adept hands, kneading my breasts, squeezing and working the flesh with a firm touch. Not hurting me, as promised. His hands pin me and prevent me from moving in any way he doesn't wish to allow.

But I want more.

"Soon," he says.

Instead of being outraged that he read my desire to feel his mouth on my flesh, I groan out his name.

It's the sound of a woman whose body talks to her, telling her with a relentless shift of her hips and rubbing together of her thighs that she needs something. And that something is within reach, if she could just figure out how to grasp it.

Adriel ends his unhurried exploration of my chest and slides his hands down my ribcage. The warmth he leaves behind keeps the cool air at bay. The mingling of our harsh breathing and the faint song of night from the woods around Kinloch are all I hear.

"Perfection," Adriel says, and I squirm with exhilaration at the words.

His hands trace my hips, coming to rest on my pubic bone.

"I can smell you, Lauren."

I hear him pull in air, a deep inhalation to fill his nostrils and lungs with the scent of my skin and the smell of my arousal.

His fingers brush over the top of my mound and he uses one hand to pin my hip while the other continues to explore. A finger traces my outer lips, and then skitters away to play in the creases where my legs join.

"Dammit, Adriel, will you touch me already?" The more he delays, the more my need for him climbs. Moisture leaks from the aching well in the center of my body.

I'd give anything to see his eyes right now and how they look at me.

A single fingertip parts my inner folds and traces up, then down, circling the place I need him most. To keep my restless hands busy, I reach for the one he's using to tease me. His hand leaves my hip and knocks it away before I can touch him.

"If you really want something to do," he says, his voice a low purr, "you can touch your breasts. Go on. Touch them the way I did."

I moan softly at the directive, and do as he suggested. The moment I close my fingers on the stiff peak of my nipples, Adriel slips two fingers inside me.

My slick hole welcomes the invasion, clenching greedily at his digits. Adriel moves them with slow deliberation, running them in a tight circle, pressing them into my walls with a thorough touch.

I whimper and shudder, not allowing myself any reservations at how easily aroused and responsive I am to both of our hands.

A third finger joins the other two, and he pumps them in and out at a slow but steady pace.

He pries my right hand away from my breast. When I open my mouth to protest, he leans down and takes the nipple into his mouth. I lose my chastisement to another moan of his name.

My fingers dig into his silken locks and he responds with vigor, sucking and licking the tender flesh. I'm not conscious of what words fall from my lips, just that I hear my voice urging him on.

His hand returns to pin my hip down and I protest with a small growl of my own when he stops me from rocking myself against his hand.

"Lauren?"

"Yes?" My response is whispered, desperate.

"Feed me."

Adriel

I crush my lips against hers, none of the gentle kisses from earlier left inside me. My lust rages, and I take it out on her mouth.

She sucks in a shocked intake of breath, and with the parting of her lips, I thrust my tongue into her mouth, probing and sweeping in time with the rhythm of my fingers within her slick folds.

She clutches my hair in both fists and holds me to her. I grin even as I continue the onslaught, sucking on her tongue, then her lips, thrusting into her again and again.

I draw the power of her will, need, and lust from her mouth and swallow it down. She gives and gives to me, and I don't let up. I need this from her. I need her to feed me her strong will, her desire for me, and her bold energy. I lift my mouth only long enough for her to gasp a deep breath and then I seal her lips to mine again.

She grabs the wrist of the hand I'm using to fuck her and wraps her fingers tight around it while the other continues to grip my hair.

My lovely goddess-in-the-moonlight matches my thrusts, rocking her hips, grinding herself against my fingers. I press my thumb against her clit, driving her into a frenzy. All I have to do now is hold myself steady and let her set the pace. My hand is coated in her juices, and her power.

I fist a hand into her hair so I can keep her under control. She's making the most delightful sounds, and I sense how close she is to her orgasm.

"Adriel." When I lift my mouth long enough for her to suck in more air, she cries my name again.

The second time she says it, I capture it with my mouth and draw it into me, swallowing it whole.

Names have power. With my true name on her lips, she breathes magic into me, the same way her hands have shaped my flesh.

I'm still swallowing her words when she shatters on my hand, tight tunnel clenching and pulling at my fingers, pulsing with the energy I need from her.

"Give me everything, my blossom. Bloom for me."

I'm not draining her power; I'm receiving the gift and reinforcing it. Our linked bodies, lips, mouth, hands, and drenched entrance holding fingers deep, create an endless circuit for the energy to feed our power. Hers, a mystery to us both in a world long moved on from magic. Mine, built on years of natural skill and study and struggling to wake fully after centuries of sleep.

I could take it.

I could drain her dry and leave her a husk of a woman, to die here under the thumbnail moon. Death magic is not a mystery to me, but I find it unnecessary outside of dueling.

I don't want to duel Lauren.

I want to devour her.

Lauren's body goes limp, except for her heaving chest. She releases a ragged sigh and I loosen my hold on her so she can catch her breath. Lifting my mouth from hers, I lick away the tears leaking from both eyes. Tears are another kind of power, but I prefer our lust and fulfillment.

With care, I slip my fingers from her heat and bring them to my mouth. The sweet tang of her on my tongue mingles with the salt of the tears I lapped up. I close my eyes with a satisfied sigh.

The only good thing about being stuck in this state of ridiculous arousal for centuries is that it doesn't physically hurt. If my cock were flesh right now, it would burst from the strength of the desire I have for this woman.

"Delicious," I murmur in my native tongue.

"Hmm?"

Lauren's drowsy inquiry reminds me I'm not alone. After centuries, at last I am not alone. Old habits of keeping myself company die hard.

"You said you'd tell me a story."

With a last lingering look at her beauty, I cover her body with the blanket she brought and tuck it around her. My current state doesn't offer enough body heat to warm her against the chill, and I cannot afford for her to grow ill.

"Will you hear how Cardle's great enemy, the leader of the Wolf Head clan, became the devil dog you worked on today?"

"Yes!" Her voice is stronger, and the flushed heat from our passion slowly drains from her cheeks. "But his name's McCardle."

"Bah! He took that name later to fit in with the Scots. He was first known as Cardle, the second best magic user of all our people."

"Who was the first?"

"Me, 'tis certain."

"If it was you, why are you a lion?"

Ah, a well-placed blow. I snarl at her.

"That's another story and one not for trade tonight. Now, do you wish to know about the devil dog or not?"

"I'm sorry," she says in a meek voice. A meekness I do not believe for one moment. This woman sings out in my blood, saying she can be as immovable as a block of the granite she loves so well, should she set her mind to it.

I spin the yarn for her, though I am rusty in the ways of a loremaster. It's been long and long and long since I had anyone to tell my tales. The birds stopped listening centuries ago, and the moon never answers me anymore.

A more responsive audience I have not had in some time. She asks questions and makes appreciative sounds in the right places, and does not complain when I slip a hand under her quilt to test her attention.

As a reward for that, I find a more imaginative use for my tongue and bring her to a second vigorous climax.

Lauren

"Listen to me, Lauren," Adriel says before he sends me back to my own bed. "Tomorrow I want you to bring me something special. Something I've never had."

The caress of his voice sends my imagination into overdrive. *What is it he's never had?*

He shoves my clothes into my hands since I can't find them with my eyes still closed.

"Huh?" I fumble my clothes on and wrap myself in the duvet. It's so chilly I can't believe it's springtime. Scottish spring and Joplin, Missouri spring are not the same season.

"I want you to bring me a bowl of ice cream. I'll put a note in the library for you to tell you what flavor."

"What?" My forehead creases in confusion. *Did my imaginary crush just ask for ice cream?*

"Ice cream. Library. Note."

"You are so weird."

"I said I would prove myself. When you find my note and you find the ice cream in the freezer, you'll know."

"How do *you* know there's ice cream in the freezer?"

"Cook bought it and then she forgot. It's still there. You wanted me to prove I am no dream figment."

Adriel kisses me and I taste myself on his lips.

"God this dream gets weirder all the time."

"You did not think it so weird when you came for me tonight." His voice turns husky. "You seemed to think it quite pleasant then. Do you not find our time together worthwhile? Or is it only *weird?*"

"Weirdly hot," I say and can't stop the smile that cracks my face. "So, *so* hot."

"Good night," he says, and I can tell he's still annoyed at being called weird. He speaks a word and my ears pop.

I'm dropped back in my bed, twisted up in the duvet and clutching my pillow to my chest. My satiated body tells my brain to shut up and let it sleep, and I drop into a boneless heap.

No one said I couldn't use the library, but I haven't specifically been invited inside any part of the manor aside from my little tower. I'm strictly outdoor help, it seems.

There's no reading material in my room. Time to remedy that.

This morning I resisted coming downstairs to the library first thing, refusing to follow the orders of some wild dream creation. My resolve lasted until after breakfast. When Cook isn't looking, I slip into the main part of the manor. The part I've been locked out of since I arrived.

Floor to ceiling shelves take up two walls of the library. There's one of those fancy wheeled ladders like you see in movies, so people can reach the top shelves. The slight charred-wood and vanilla scent of old books lingers. I could lose myself in here.

Small stacks of books dot the long table in the center of the room, and I gravitate toward it to browse the titles. At the far end of the table, a thick volume with gilt lettering catches my eye.

Statuary of Scottish Forts, Castles, and Manor Houses by John Mc-Gregor. I scoop the book up, and turn to the table of contents. Kinloch Manor is listed on page three hundred thirty-three. I turn fragile pages with care, my heart hammering. I've seen a lot of books on the history of gargoyles and grotesques, but this title is new to me.

A thick, cream-colored sheet of paper falls out of the book and flutters to the table, face-up. Heavy block letters catch my eye.

LAUREN. RUM AND RAISIN.

My heart skips a beat before blood roars in my ears and sweat slicks my palms.

I pinch the inside of my arm. "Ow!"

Not a dream.

I pick the note up with a shaking hand, rattling the paper. I can't stop looking at the message. *Rum and raisin* echoes around my head in an endless loop.

"I didn't write this." My uttered words crack and echo in the high-ceilinged room. Freaked, I shove the paper into the book and slam the cover closed, not using care now.

I flee toward the kitchen, clutching the book against my chest.

When I shove my way through the door, I startle Cook. We stare at each other in shock.

"I'm uh, I…Did you leave a note for me in the library?" My voice sounds accusatory, but I don't care.

"I've left nothing for ye anywhere," she says, still studying my face.

"And McCardle? Did he leave me a note?"

"*Lord* McCardle has left ye nothing."

"I need to look in the freezer," I blurt out and push past her. Behind me, she *harumphs* at my American rudeness, but makes no move to stop me from invading the pantry.

I pull open the lid on the chest freezer.

With one hand, I dig in the contents of the freezer until I find a little carton of ice cream wedged in a corner.

Rum and raisin.

I drop it like it's on fire. The lid slams down and I stumble out of the pantry to find Cook stirring a boiling pot on the stove.

"Is there anyone else working in the manor? Besides you and the groundskeeper?"

"The weekly maid," she says. "And you." The word 'you' comes out of her with such disdain that I step back.

My god, *someone* is here, and they've drugged me. They've drugged me with a hallucinogen and they've...what have they done that triggered the weird, intense sex dreams?

"But no one else is here? No one is visiting or staying in a guest room o-or anything?"

Cook taps her spoon on the side of the pan and sets it on the counter. She faces me, and a brief flash of annoyance crosses her expression before she smooths her face into a blank mask.

"What have ye seen?"

"What makes you think I've seen anything?"

We lock stares.

"Don't go out of yer room after sundown," she says, voice low and demanding. "The manor is...haunted. Ye'll fall into evil if you let hi—" She stops, clears her throat. "If you aren't careful."

"Haunted!" I blurt and almost laugh. It's not a funny ha-ha laugh. What's bubbling up inside me resembles hysteria.

Because I haven't been dreaming, have I? And if not, I've been hallucinating and someone in this manor is responsible. Maybe it's in my food. Maybe Cook put it there.

"Haunted." She turns back to the stove, and pretends I'm not standing in her kitchen on the verge of a nervous breakdown.

I run up the stairs and I don't stop running until I collapse on the bed in my tower room, gasping for breath. Conversations with Adriel invade my thoughts and I sift through the words in search of clues. My brain created this mad mashup of man and grotesque and gave it a name. Of course it latched onto my favorite statue out of the seven in Kinloch's collection. Is this how I'm coping with being drugged and...what? Assaulted? Do I know it happened?

Does Cook really believe Kinloch is haunted, or is she trying to scare me?

I toy with the idea that the equipment safety measures failed and I plummeted from the manor walls and cracked my head. Maybe I'm comatose in a hospital bed somewhere, producing fever dreams.

Too many questions, and too few answers.

Once my wind returns, I pace the little bedroom in a burst of anxious energy, driven by frantic thoughts. My footsteps ring hollow on the stone floor.

There's no one to talk to about what's happening. Cook proved useless, I rarely see the groundskeeper, and McCardle only comes every few days to check my progress. Unless he comes back after I've ingested whatever they've given me. But why?

"I have to go. I can't be here right now."

The words hang in the oppressive air of my tiny room.

I decide to stay in town for the weekend and pack toiletries and clothes in my backpack. Spotting the McGregor book on the bed, I zip it into the front compartment of my bag and make my escape.

Outside, I can't help but look up at Adr—, I mean, the man-lion who hovers well above the entrance, seeing everything and everyone who comes and goes. If only he could tell me Kinloch's secrets.

Lauren.

I whirl around, but the courtyard is empty. I've definitely given myself the creeps and need to get out of here.

Adriel

Lauren fled. No other word best describes what happened when she found my laboriously written note and the book I left for her. English is not my first (or even third) language and writing in it is quite the challenge. I first learned those clunky letters when Cook was a child, when we were friends. She had not yet formed her angry opinions of me under the influence of Cardle.

I suppose I will not be getting ice cream tonight. A fair disappointment to say the least.

With the sun traveling the sky, there's nothing I can do to prevent her leaving. Has she gone for good? I do not believe so, as she's left her beloved tools behind.

Cardle returns to the manor shortly before sunset, no doubt informed by Cook of Lauren's departure and her strange behavior this morning. He rarely sets foot here after dark, not in the past century or so.

He dares to visit my rooftop after the moon rises. I crouch in the darkest corner near the north tower and pull the shroud of night around my form. He cannot be allowed to see the progress of my transformation, brought forth by Lauren's magical hands. Not until it's complete, not until I am fully prepared.

Cardle must continue to believe I am confined to my prison.

Which is accurate still. For now. Lauren must finish what she started.

He speaks in the old tongue. "I know you hear me, you beastly rogue. Stay away from my little artist and leave her to do her work."

Change comes. I do not need to speak to communicate with the bastard.

"Leave it. There is nothing you can do and scaring the woman with your little games will gain you nothing." He chuckles, and my ears prick at the underlying hint of nervousness in it.

He's still nettled that I drove his fifth wife insane and scared most of the staff away at long last. Something *has* changed. No children remain to perpetuate his line. Cardle will have to work harder to assume the identity of an heir to inherit the manor from himself upon 'his' death.

Now only the two of us remain, locked in our immortality together. None of his children over the centuries had his talents, and so they lived out their mortal lives as any would.

Except for those he sacrificed to his needs. Power is never free.

Change comes. I repeat it to annoy him. *I saw the crow speaking to the raven in the seventh hour just last month. Ill tidings to you, Cardle.*

He fumes.

For too long, he used his power for dark deeds and selfish purposes. But once the lightning struck Selene, his protective Ward of Seven started to decay. He seeks to replace her, but the amount of time that's passed with no new trapped soul in place has created a vacuum. An opportunity.

All who wield magic know if you hold the negative backlash at bay, as he has done for centuries, it will slap all the harder when you meet it at last.

The aura of his power appears faded, like clothing that's been washed too many times.

If he knew just how pale, how thin, the color surrounding him is, he would never dare this visit to my domain. Night on this side of the Veil belongs to me, though he has walked here before. Not often, but he has always enjoyed gloating over his victory.

Perhaps he did win the original battle, though not the war.

Cardle holds out a hand. A small flame hovers above it. While it is not enough for him to pierce my shadows, the light glows bright enough for me to see the sheen of sweat on his forehead. I grin in triumph. All of this costs him more than he can truly afford.

"Accept your fate. Give up, sink into the stone, and do not return. The others never resisted, and your fight has ever been nothing but your inability to accept your own doom."

Let him rant.

I ceased having concern for the state of my trapped soul quite some time ago, but my new hopes continue to unfurl from the center of my dead stone heart. After so long, this must come to an end.

One way or another.

My real hope lies with Lauren, with the idea that her hands may return me to a fully human state, even if I never cross back from the purgatory Cardle cursed me to inhabit. If I could just be a man again, just one more time...

My fingers flex with the memory of the delicate curve of Lauren's neck, the way her sun-kissed skin prickled at my touch. I mull over thoughts of her from head to toe. The way her hair catches glimmers of fire when the sun finds the burnished strands mixed in her deep brown locks, the play of her muscles as they clench in pleasure.

Once, I might have behaved as Cardle and taken everything from her, willing or not. My prison taught me much about the man I was, the man I might have been, and the man I might be yet.

"She won't stay. Her time here will be a mere blink of an eye compared to our life spans. You'll be forgotten again. And alone." The corners of his mouth twist into a mocking smile and still I resist the bait.

Tuning him out, I focus on my memories of Lauren.

The stench of his nervous sweat lingers long after he flees my rooftop lair.

Lauren

For two restless nights, I pace my little hotel room, asking myself what was real and what was a fever dream. *Was* I drugged? With what, and why? Is it a sick prank?

Maybe I need to talk with McCardle, but accusing his staff of drugging me without proof, well...I hesitate to do it.

I need this job.

My future depends on completing this contract to the highest standard possible. And if I fumble it, word will get around. Historic restoration can be a small community, even on a worldwide scale. I'd rather be eaten by the resident manticore—and not in the sexy way—than have my ex get wind I failed at my first independent job.

If McCardle's staff, or whoever is in on this, thinks I'm going down without a fight, they've got another thing coming.

I spend two days shopping in Bartonshire, breathing easier being at least a two hour drive from the Manor and ninety minutes from the sparsely populated Kinloch Village. I've bought bottled water and food to last a couple of weeks. No way I'm eating or drinking anything at Kinloch, not even Cook's scones, until I figure out what's going on there.

Hopping behind the wheel of the Fiat, I head back to Kinloch Manor with my supplies in the boot of the car and steel in my spine. I will not allow myself to be afraid, or leave an unfulfilled contract behind me. And I sure as hell won't run away without getting my questions answered. One way or another.

"Oh, *come on!*" My heart starts hammering, but I'm not sure if it's fear or anger. Maybe both. I swallow back the lump in my throat and focus on calming my racing pulse.

Clouds cover the moon, but the rooftop torches burn bright against the inky sky bearing down. A distant high-pitched cry echoes from the woods and I flinch.

"It's only an owl," Adriel says from his corner of darkness. "And a good om—"

"You!" I jab my finger at him. "You stay back."

The only thing I ate and drank today came from the supplies I brought back yesterday and yet I've found myself on this bloody rooftop again. My bare feet dig into the soft moss, leaving deep impressions to mark my agitated path as I pace back and forth.

Did I hallucinate the note I found? I reach in my pocket and draw out the crumpled paper, an anchor for my tumultuous mind.

"You did not bring ice cream. I was looking forward to trying rum and raisin." Adriel's accent thickens with displeasure. "And you ran away."

"Who are you?"

"Adriel."

Insufferable prick!

"Not particularly. I've learned to live with it."

"Wha—"

Oh. *Ohhhh.*

"This isn't the time for dick jokes." I shove the note back into my pocket. "How are you doing this?"

He snorts. "Close your eyes."

"No." Defiance—or maybe simple adrenaline—crashes through me like a river bursting a dam. I ignore the weakness in my knees. "Do you work for McCardle?"

Adriel roars with such ferocity a breeze ruffles my hair. Even the faint night music of the forest is startled into silence.

My legs betray me and I drop to my knees, the ground shaking beneath me. *It's all part of the hallucination. Or the dream. Or whatever the hell this is.*

He spits an angry string of words in that strangely melodic accent. "Tread with care, Lauren. I have been a beast overlong now. I may forget myself."

I squash the impulse to apologize. *I'm the one owed an apology here.*

Maybe the thought is written on my face because he disagrees and curses again. "*Apology?*" If he actually was a lion, his tail would be whipping back and forth in agitation.

Uneasy silence falls between us. "Come out of the shadows and stop playing games with me."

"You aren't ready," he growls from the darkness.

"Try me."

The shadows shift, and my breath hitches in the middle of my chest. My heart flutters like a bird beating itself against the bars of a cage, and I swallow with a dry *click*.

Stone scrapes on stone, and Adriel lumbers into the far edge of the light cast by the torches.

He's beautiful. And horrifying. A figure carved by a sculptor driven mad by a deranged god.

My brain fails to translate what my eyes see, and his form jumps and flickers, that same broken projector effect from before. I swallow back bile and screw my eyes shut tight.

"Is this where I say I told you so?" he asks, his voice a rasp grinding away at sharp edges.

I squint at him with one eye, a mockery of a cheeky wink. In the warm torchlight, his face and arms appear covered in fine dust. His hair is black ink spilling across gray-and-tan dappled shoulders. The entirety of his chest is the same dark shade of stone as the sculptures adorning the manor's walls. His humanity ends at the waist, and becomes beast posing as man, standing on two powerful back legs. A lion's tail curls around his ankle, the tip brushing his paw in short swipes that speak of irritation. Or is it shyness?

The form solidifies, and my other eye creaks open a fraction of an inch. His image wavers, then settles. My mind wants to fight about whether I am in fact dreaming, or hallucinating while wide awake.

"You are tiresome," Adriel says, and sighs with such bone-weary gusto that I expect him to collapse.

"What *are* you?" I wince at my rudeness. Maybe he's the victim of some horrid, incurable disease I've never heard of, some form of leprosy that turns a person to stone instead of causing them to rot.

Really, Lauren? You think this guy suffers from some kind of disease that gives him an enormous stone hard-on?

And now I don't know where to settle my eyes. If I look at his feet, then I'm staring at that deformed part of him. If I stare into his eyes, the only other part of him with color—a color I can't make out from this distance—then I'm obviously avoiding looking at the elephant in the room.

Elephant! My mind voice yammers, and I bite my bottom lip, looking at the turret over his left shoulder.

"Honestly, woman. All you ever seem to worry about is my cock."

"I—what? Wh—No, I..."

I what? It's not like he's wrong.

"What am I?" He snarls and smacks one hand on a stony thigh. The flat slap of flesh on rock echoes across the rooftop. "I'm cursed."

Adriel

*T*his maddening woman.

Tonight her doubts and worries fail to blow apart my magic. I admire her determination to see this through. To see *me*. The brief time she spent away from the manor seems to have allowed both of us to rebuild our strength.

"Cursed?" Her right eyebrow lifts, easy-to-read skepticism evident on her face. "How are you cursed?"

"You are full of questions." I shuffle toward the mossy bed I created. My stone legs never tire, but the chance to sit near Lauren draws me.

She steps back and I repress a growl at her unfounded suspicion. The answers she desires stick in my throat, lodged there by Cardle's magic. If I could speak of it to her, I would.

"You talk to the stone when you work as if they can hear you," I say, hoping to distract her, but also to hear more of her work. The love of it bleeds into her voice when she speaks, the next best thing to being the true object of such affection.

"*You* seem to be hearing me." Her eyes glitter with suspicion. "You know a lot about what goes on here."

Cheeky wench.

"Tell me of your trip to town."

Lauren takes this as an excuse to blister my ears with her accusations that someone in the house—me, she implies—has poisoned her food and caused her to have 'hallucinations'. *Drugged*, she calls it.

I perch on the edge of the bench with care. My back legs aren't meant for human positions. She paces back and forth, venting her wrath at me. I sympathize with her. The Veil is an odd place to inhabit.

"Peace, woman. Sit with me." I gesture to the space beside me and repress amusement at the outrage on her face. "Please."

Her expression says she will refuse me. Maybe even launch into a new attack. But the curiosity that's always under her surface bubbles up and she perches on the end of the bench, out of my reach. Or so she thinks.

The weight of her gaze lands on me and I turn my head to find her staring at the stone wings protruding from my back. Cardle's little joke on me; there's no dignity in these tiny wings.

"How...that's not poss—" She cuts off, confused. "Do they hurt?"

"No." I flex my hands, drawing her attention to them.

"Your hands are tan. Human."

"Because your touch is freeing me from the stone."

"But how?" The tremor in her voice saddens me.

How to explain magic to someone who doesn't know they have it?

"Can I touch them? The wings."

"If you wish." I look away, afraid my eyes will reveal too much. Suppose she sees the vast emptiness lurking inside me. Or glimpses my terrible longing for her and escapes Kinloch once more. I crave her touch so deeply my mouth waters. Imagine how far she would flee if I should drool on her like a slavering beast.

She rises and I hold myself steady.

If she runs, you must not give chase.

She circles behind me. Her light caress brushes the feathers sprouting from my back and a delicious shiver rips through me. She pauses, but when I grow still, her touch becomes firmer, more confident. When one wing crumbles to dust beneath her fingers, she jumps back with an alarmed yelp.

"Oh my god, did I hurt you?"

"You can't hurt me." No need to mention the gaping wound where once my soul resided. No need to allow a glimpse into my dark desire for her touch.

"Why did that happen?" She runs her fingertips over the area where the wing once bloomed. I repress a groan, lest she step away.

"Because I never had wings as a man." Or a tail, but we'll get to that later.

"There's no mark, nothing. But it's still your...skin? It's..."

"It's still stone. I am far from free. Continue."

She mutters to herself, doubt and belief at war within her. Her touch shifts to the remaining wing and after several minutes that one falls to dust as well. Hands caress my back, long strokes from shoulder blade to the base of my spine. Stone turns to skin, becoming warm and pliant.

"Unbelievable," she says.

I stay silent, and she continues wielding her magic.

My back restored to flesh, she moves to finish my shoulders. Her palms smooth their way around my shoulder blades, my collarbone, my upper arms.

Lauren's magic wavers and retreats; nothing more can be done for the night. All magic has limits. Push past those boundaries and the magic drinks deep of your life energy, sometimes to the point of death.

I lift her hand from my shoulder and kiss the palm in thanks. Her breathing hitches, and I slide my lips to the pulse in her wrist. It flutters when I press a kiss there.

"Go to your bed, Lauren." I hesitate. "I will see you tomorrow night?" The note of pleading in my voice is enough to make me cringe. I should have made it a command. Once, I had but to speak a whim and it would be answered willingly by another. Now I sound like a mewling child, begging for attention after being left alone too long.

And I need her gone. Now. With her delicate scent in my nostrils, I may forget patience. With her warm touch, I may remember too well what we shared before she became afraid.

Her lips purse, a question ready to drop from them. Hunger roars through me. My gaze locks on her mouth, and her tongue darts out to moisten her bottom lip. *Enough.* I squeeze her hand and whisper the words to send her back across the Veil, into her own bed and a deep sleep.

Lauren

I scramble out of bed the next morning and check the pockets of the shorts I wore to sleep. A frown pulls my lips tight and draws my eyebrows together.

I knew it, nothing! There's—

My right hand fishes out the small pebble I rescued when Adriel's wings crumbled to dust at my feet. My left closes on the pinch of moss I stuck in my pocket after I fell to my knees.

Under the bright sunlight streaming through my little window, I examine the items in my palm. I don't need to compare the pebble to know it matches the grotesques on the manor walls. Pinching the moss between my fingers, I study it at all angles. Holding it to my nose, I sniff the piece of Adriel's world I stole. The sharp earthy scent fills my nostrils.

Everything about it seems ordinary.

Setting both objects on the little desk, I bolt up the stairs to the rooftop. The *stone* rooftop with its stone bench. No torches, no moss. No Adriel.

Back in my bedroom, I take a long time to dress, lost deep in thought and unable to stop staring at the tiny objects on the desk. The ones that tell me I'm not dreaming or hallucinating. The questions rattle around my brain, and I stomp down the stairs, ready to question Cook again.

What if she thinks you're crazy? What if she tells her boss, your boss, that you're crazy?

Instead of going straight to the kitchen, I slip past and enter the main part of the manor and head for the central staircase. The red-eyed viper on McCardle's family crest seems to follow my progress. Cold prickles my back and seeps into my guts and I hurry to escape its baleful gaze.

Glancing around the second floor landing and seeing no one, I slip down the east hallway. Starting at the far end of the hall, I open every door that isn't locked and peer inside. Countless bedrooms and connecting dressing rooms appear unused. White dust covers create ghostly outlines of the furniture. No light shows through heavy drapes drawn across windows.

When I reach the last bedroom nearest to the staircase, I step inside. The hair on the back of my neck stands up, and I throw a nervous glance over my shoulder. A crawling sensation works its way down my spine. All I want to do is run from this room, but I swallow that down.

I slide open drawers and peek inside closets, imagining myself a spy.

Nothing.

Nothing.

More nothing.

Blowing out a breath, I turn to leave. Something above the door catches my eye. I drag a chair closer, wincing at the muffled sound of its wooden legs dragging over the rich Persian carpet, hoping Cook or the housekeeper I've never seen won't pop up to investigate. I kick off my shoes and stand on the cushion, squinting in the dim light at the design carved over the door.

Runes?

On my tiptoes, I stretch and touch the carving. An unpleasant tingling runs up my arm, a thousand tiny pinpricks. I jerk my fingers away, eyeing the engraving with suspicion.

"What are you doing there?" a voice demands from the hallway.

I jerk in surprise and flail my arms in an attempt to keep my balance. The chair tips and I crash to the floor with a yelp.

"Here now! Ye better not have broken that chair!" Cook says in a blistering scold.

What is she doing up here? I've never known her to leave her first-floor lair.

"Yeah, I'm fine, thanks." My voice trembles, but the sarcasm remains strong. I take an inventory, but I don't think I've broken any bones. Or the chair for that matter.

I shove to my feet and right the chair, ignoring Cook's deadly stare. A few deep breaths into my lungs and my hands stop shaking from my little scare.

"What is that?" I point to the rune.

"It's naught but a wee protection. 'Tis very common."

Why is she lying?

"It is not. I've studied—"

She cuts me off. "Well, ye don't know ever'thin' now do you, Little Miss Smarty? Why are ye not outside workin'?" The madder she gets, the thicker her accent becomes.

Chastised, I slink from the room under her watchful eye, cheeks flaming in belated embarrassment at being caught poking around in the guest rooms.

After I hustle back to the rooftop and send my tool kit over the wall, I use the bosun's chair to lower myself over the west side of the manor. Time to work on the devil dog.

Lost in the work, my mind wanders to Adriel. The story he told me of the human clan chief who crossed the man he calls Cardle runs through my head like a short film. I murmur reassuring words to the devil dog, conscious that Adriel will claim to know this private conversation.

With intention, I lay my hands on the grotesque and concentrate. I recall how it felt when Adriel's wings crumbled between my fingers and try to channel that into the devil dog.

Nothing happens. My skin stays cool to the touch, the warmth in my hands nothing more than what I would normally experience while working with stone. I examine my fingers, my palms, the backs of my hands. Adriel claims there's magic in them, in me, but I can't manage to pull it out at will.

A low, rhythmic *chug-chug* catches my attention and my eyes are drawn to the thin stretch of roadway that peeps out between the trees. A tractor putters past, the distance between Kinloch and the road so great that it looks like a model toy being propelled by a child's hand.

I close my eyes and breathe in the peace and solitude. This job suits me well, letting me work alone, at my own pace, doing things the way I like them. Luckily, my client is cooperative with my vision and my pace.

Now if I could get the cantankerous man-lion on board with my very *not fired* goals.

Cook hides from me when I make my way to the kitchen for lunch. I slap a sandwich together, toss some crisps on the plate, and stomp back upstairs, using the noise to convey my whereabouts. Now she won't think I'm sneaking around again.

I desperately want to sneak around again.

Instead, I'm on the rooftop eating my lunch and peering over the side, examining Adriel. Under the sun, he remains unchanged from the great stone lion I laid eyes on the day I arrived. Under the moonlight, well...

Curses, magic, living stone.

Maybe I should try to enjoy feeling relieved I'm not being drugged, for one thing. But all of this is so much to take in. Part of me wants to find a closet to hide in, where I can curl up into a ball and never think about any of it again.

Or almost any of it.

I tilt my head back to soak up the sunlight and close my eyes. Thoughts of nights spent on this roof feel safer in the daytime, so I lose myself in the memory of Adriel's hands roaming my body. The intense pleasure he created inside of me with his hands and mouth.

Of how embarrassing it is that I surrendered myself to a stranger so easily, thinking it was a dream.

I'm still not ready to forgive him for being real, even though he never lied about it.

I think of the cautious way he treated me last night, how his wings crumbled to nothing, how his skin warmed under my touch and gained the deep tan of a man who has spent a lot of time outdoors.

My fingers flex, recalling the way his muscles relaxed under my hands and the soft sighs I'm not even sure he was aware of releasing while I worked to free him.

So many questions crowd my mind, I don't know where to start.

I think I'll be too wound up to fall asleep, and if I can't sleep, how will I find Adriel tonight? I drum my fingers on top of the blanket, staring up at the ceiling. How does this work? The sun set two hours ago, and I hopped into bed early.

My eyes pinch closed and I inhale a slow deep breath through my nose and hold it.

One, two, three, four.

I release the breath, counting to four again. I repeat this several times, and I'm about to give up when I feel it. A sharp tug, deep in the pit of my stomach.

My eyes fly open, and I can almost hear Adriel's exasperated sigh.

Relax, he says. *You have only to relax and I will do the rest.*

So I try again and I'm rewarded with the spring breeze whispering across my face and neck. My eyes snap open and take in the first of the night's stars twinkling above me.

Oh, cool, I want to say, but hold back. I remind myself that I'm still too unsure what's happening to let my guard down.

I leap up, and wiggle my toes, enjoying the soft, springy feel of the mossy bed under my bare feet. Biting my lip, I repress a delighted smile. As if I can hide anything from Adriel, who seems to know my thoughts all too often for comfort.

Caution, remember?

Tonight he doesn't hide from me in the shadows. He stands where I stood earlier today when I examined him in the sunshine. I move to his side, and find him staring at the empty pedestal he inhabits during the day. He says nothing, but there's a strange cloud around him, a mood I can't quite grasp.

"Adriel?"

"My arms, please," he says, and extends his left arm without looking at me.

The hand is normal, flesh. His wrist appears banded, and I squint, trying to get a better understanding of what I'm seeing. His arm twists, and he grabs my hand, tightening his fingers around mine. My heart flutters and I take a deep breath.

"What did this?" I ask, touching the mottled flesh with my free hand.

"You." He shrugs a shoulder. "You grabbed my wrists when I drank you in."

"Drank me?"

"When I—"

"Oh, yeah! I got it!" I say, so loud the words echo over the rooftop. "I mean, I remember now, thanks."

"Oh no, Lauren, thank *you*." He chuckles, and I would slap his bicep, but I'd probably break my hand on the stone.

"Arms," I say, throwing him a dark look.

He's stopped looking at me and returned to staring at his empty perch.

"Moody."

He doesn't respond to the provocation.

I massage his wrist and watch the mottled skin change color. The gray fades away, and the warmth bleeds into his flesh. It's impossible to look away from the magic happening right before my eyes.

When I finish his left arm, he says, "Thank you, blossom," and continues staring into the night. By now I'm uneasy with his ongoing silence, so I don't call him out for using his special nickname for me. Which he absolutely should *not* say in that low, sexy voice.

"Tell me a story," I say instead, rubbing his right wrist with cramping fingers.

"What story would you hear?"

"Tell me about your curse."

His head swivels toward me, and his face twists in a rictus of pain. Cords pop out along his neck and a sound erupts from deep in his throat.

My hands tighten around his forearm. *God, is he having a stroke? Or turning back to stone?*

"Adriel?"

He shakes his head and looks away.

"A different story then. Anything." I loosen my hands. "You choose."

Another moment passes, then he heaves out a breath. "So I shall."

He points out a large cluster of stars with his free hand, and tells me the most outrageous, graphic story about the origins of the universe.

"And here, you see," he sweeps his hand across the night sky. "Countless children of light birthed from that joining of the Night Mistress to her lover."

"Adriel!" This time I do hit him on the arm, the light slap landing on warm flesh instead of rock, and his throaty laugh causes something deep in my core to tighten. "That's the Milky Way, not a giant goddess's vagina!"

And even as I say it, I think his story is a lovelier explanation than anything modern science offers.

His heated expression hints that he has more to teach me about cosmic romance if I am willing to learn.

Driven by a need to put space between us, I pace the entire edge of the rooftop, walking next to the chest-high wall, flexing my hands and shaking them out.

He wears a knowing smile when I return to his side, and I don't protest when he takes my hand and kisses the palm. He places it against his cheek, eyes closed, and pulls a deep breath into his nostrils. He's breathing me in and soaking me up, like he's taking me inside himself because it could be the last time we ever meet and he has to make the most of it.

I brush my thumb lightly over his full bottom lip and his eyelids snap open. The irises are a beautiful slate gray, and burn so hot, I take a step back. In a flash, the heat in his gaze shutters and he releases my hand.

I want to tell him I didn't mean to back away, but how do I just open my mouth and say *Sorry, this magic thing is new to me, plus I don't want you to have the wrong idea about me since I thought you were a slightly wonderful, slightly weird dream, and really I just want you to do all those things to me again before I leave this place forever?*

Yeah, I'm not ready to make a bigger fool out of myself.

To clear my head, I give it a little shake and run my eyes over Adriel from head to toe.

He's looking better, stronger. Vibrant.

"It was easier when you were not able to look at me so," he says.

I cock my head, uncertain of his meaning.

"Have you seen one?"

I'm thrown off-balance by the shift in topic. "Seen what?"

"A lion. A *real* lion. Are they as hideous as my form hints?"

"Hideous?" And it hits me that of course he's probably never seen a real lion. "No, they're majestic. Beautiful."

His eyes gleam in response. He tosses his head and the movement flips his wavy locks back over his shoulders in a move any supermodel would envy.

And now I've created a monster.

I could make a lion pride joke. But if I had to explain it, it wouldn't be funny.

"Your color looks good," I say as an alternative. "We should take care of your chest." I reach out to place my palm against his breastbone and he recoils, intercepting my hand.

"No!"

I flinch at his tone, and his expression softens. His thumb strokes the pulse point in my wrist and gooseflesh breaks out along my arm.

"Not yet. I remain uncertain what might happen should my heart begin beating again. I may well turn to dust and crumble away."

Adriel

L auren's mouth drops open. "H-how can your heart not be beat-ing?"

My magic whispers to me. I hear her unspoken question, *could someone be that warm and not have a heartbeat?*

And I want to tell her *stone lions shouldn't come to life and transform into men at all, but here we are.*

"Would you really turn to dust?"

"I am quite old," I say, and flash a smile to lighten the mood. In truth, I have forgotten how old I am. I do not know whether I will indeed disintegrate into dust or simply fade away when she finishes her task of restoring my humanity.

It may prove a relief to have done with it all. To crumble beneath her fingers, the same way my wings dissolved under her touch. I watched their remains blow away in the breeze after she departed. How long will it take me to be lifted into the wind and scattered to the four corners once she is done?

"How old?"

"What is the year?" I used to keep track, but after so many endless centuries, it became a dull practice and I gave it up.

"Twenty twenty-five."

I snort in surprise and calculate. "I am currently seven hundred and sixty-nine."

Lauren's expression shifts into a mix of horror and disbelief. And pity. She's stuttering something, but I have no wish to listen to more questions and doubts tonight.

"We shall start on legs tomorrow. Sleep well, Lauren."

I send her away in the midst of her next question, and make sure she's in a restorative sleep. My blossom might very well storm her way back across the Veil if left to her own devices, and I am too weary to prevent it. All this transformation simultaneously rebuilds and drains me. Magic requires balance; it gives and takes in equal measure.

It would be less wearying if I could have even a sip of her, but she remains cautious.

Silly modern humans with their funny ideas about sex. The monotheistic religions have done them no favors in transforming natural acts of gratification into shameful sins.

My Lauren needs to be shown once more that she is made for giving and receiving pleasure in equal measure. One day soon, she will not need to hide behind the idea that it's somehow wrong to enjoy herself with me.

Has Cardle hired this pretty little morsel to stir my lust after all this time, to distract me from his fading power? I twitch a hand, dismissing the thought. Whatever Cardle has done, is doing, he would never knowingly offer me such dazzling company. He prefers I starve.

And he has become so magic-blind, she may as well be invisible.

If the last view I have in this world is Lauren's ecstasy, I will gladly take it with me into whatever lies beyond. Even if it ends with me as a pile of rubble at her feet, it will have been a good end. And it certainly would not be the one Cardle hoped for me. He would see me on the wall another thousand years if he could.

I picture my end coming at the hands of Lauren and throw my head back, bellowing laughter.

The next time we meet, Lauren does not even greet me before she points to the bench and says, "Sit."

I sniff in disdain. Sit, indeed. "I am not a pet to be commanded."

"Just do it."

I perch on the edge of the bench, and turn my face to the sky. The fattened moon, a sliver when Lauren first arrived, hangs above the keep wall, not even half-full. Time in the Veil is no different than time in Cardle's daylight world, but I can't help the feeling that Lauren has been with me longer than the moon's phases reveal.

"Tell me a story," I say, turning the tables on her.

She sits cross-legged before me, examining my feet. If these twisted appendages can rightly be called that.

Her rich walnut-colored hair is pinned up in a messy bun, and I stare at the curve of her neck where her pulse throbs. I quash the impulse to touch the freckle at the top of her spine, unwilling to send her running before her work begins. Instead, I inhale her scent in one slow breath so she won't notice. She showered before she traveled over and smells of the air after a rainstorm. Beneath that lingers a trace of something that is all Lauren: a hint of minerals, the whiff of a summer night's breeze, and her light womanly musk.

Her hands go to work on my sorry excuse for a foot.

"Story," I say.

"What about?"

I want to know about her, but she is ever a reluctant witness, so I choose a better starting point, one I know she will enjoy.

"Tell me about," I form the unfamiliar words with care, "architecture. And sculpting classes." The flash of excitement in her runs from her hands into the stone of my foot, and the pins and needles sensation steals my breath. It's the first thing I've felt there in centuries.

Her voice washes over me, and I keep my gaze on her shoulders and bent head. Through her thin shirt, I watch her muscles flex with the effort of her work. She caresses my foot, and when she falls silent I can hear her callused hands rasp over the stone.

"I can't decide if I prefer the painted version of Greek statues, or the all-white," she says, bringing me back to the discussion.

We debate the merits of color, and I long to show her my mother's dye pots for wool. But those rainbow-hued treasures are lost to my past. Only the present, and being in it with Lauren, holds meaning now.

When my foot emerges, she exhales in a rush and leans back, rolling her shoulders. My eyes lock onto hers when she looks up with a radiant smile.

If it could beat, my heart would have skipped.

"Tougher than I thought it would be," she says. She tickles the bottom of my freed foot, but I don't feel it. Not yet.

My foot appears made of flexible stone, no longer encased in a misshapen form.

"The lower leg." I look away from her lovely face and start counting the infinite stars above our heads. "Please," I add.

I coax more stories as she works.

It's been years, but once Cook left a magazine open in the library. It advised how you might get to know someone better. I dig in my memory for the right questions to ask.

"Where were you born?" and "Tell me of your childhood" and "Are you a registered voter?" come bubbling to the surface. So I ask.

I don't know what a registered voter is—*are you running for office, Adriel?*—but my probing gains me more crumbs of information to feed my curiosity about *her*.

"Why is it called Misery?"

She laughs up at my frown with sparkling eyes and corrects me. Ah, not misery after all. *Miz-ur-ree.* I practice the word in my mind.

Her favorite song changes with her mood.

"No, I won't sing for you," she says when I ask. "And you'd thank me for that if you'd ever heard me sing."

Music. Oh, I have missed music. Cook keeps everything interesting locked in her bedroom, and with the rune in place over the doorway, I may know nothing from within.

With my thoughts turning to Cook, a shooting star plummets past. My dead heart lurches. *Omen.*

"Lauren?"

"Hmm?" She's rubbing the stone of my thigh, concentration creasing her forehead.

"Be careful. With Cook and Cardle, that is. Avoid them when you can."

She stops working and slants her gaze up at me, her eyebrows drawn together.

"Just once, believe in me." I cannot stop the harsh tone behind the words. The centuries of animosity toward Cardle, and the decades of Cook's betrayals, burn through my veins.

I wrap a hand around the back of her neck and rub my thumb along her jaw. Her pupils dilate and warmth blooms in my latent heart.

"It'll take some time to get your legs freed, I think." She's changing the subject, but I allow it, if only to avoid more talk of curses and ancient enemies.

"I have nothing but time."

She does not, of course. Her lifespan counts an infinitesimal spark against the dark night of my longevity.

Lauren returns to her efforts, and picks up the thread of her life story, spinning a new tale for me. My eyes stay locked on the moon as it moves across the sky, until I feel her energy wane.

If I did not lift her from the ground and settle her beside me on the bench, she would continue until she drained every drop of her essence into the work. She calls it "being in the zone" when she speaks of her favorite projects.

Her favorites before she came to me, that is.

Lauren shivers. I draw her against my side, leaving my arm draped around her shoulder. She fits so perfectly, she might have been carved to match me.

I tip her chin up and press my lips to hers, a close-mouthed kiss, restrained. A kiss of gratitude. Her head tilts a fraction of an inch, and I slide my hand to the nape of her neck, deepening the kiss. My hand stays loose, giving her space to pull away if she chooses.

But then she makes that small contented moan deep in her throat.

Lauren

Adriel's lips part, and I answer his desire with my own, allowing his tongue to explore my open mouth. His arm tightens around my shoulders, drawing me close. The warmth of him keeps the evening chill at bay. My shivering has nothing to do with the night air and everything to do with the way my body answers his call.

He lifts his mouth, leaving only a whisper of space between our lips.

"You will stay in your room tomorrow night and rest," he says, tone softening the order. "I will not call for you."

"What if I call for you?" I ask, and blush. I have called for him in the past. I called his name to the heavens when he had me spread beneath him and kissed me in a far more intimate way.

"Don't be shy with me, Lauren. You are free to indulge at will." The intensity in his eyes spark a fire low in my belly.

My brain slowly works its way through his words, but I'm prevented from having to respond by another deep kiss.

"And you have more work ahead of you that will require both your energy, and your fortitude against bashfulness." A smile curves his lips. His hand closes over one of mine, and drops them both into his lap.

He wraps our hands around the thick base of his stone erection, and his eyes gleam with mischief.

"You—that's...what do you think you're doing?"

"Teasing you, 'tis certain. It is quite easy to do, and you fluster magnificently."

He shuts his eyes and it's as if he's closed a curtain. A fist squeezes my heart in warning.

The question I've been ignoring bubbles out of my mouth, safe to present itself now that his eyes are hidden. "Do you like me because I'm the first woman you've seen in, well, forever?" The knot in my throat lodges midway and won't go down.

His low chuckle vibrates in the marrow of my bones. Lips brush my cheek and he whispers, "Who says I like you?"

I jerk as if I've been slapped and try to pull away.

He tightens his hold on me and his smile fades, replaced by a flash of chagrin.

He presses his forehead to mine and the tips of our noses touch. "Should a hundred other women parade across my rooftop, I will have eyes for only one."

His kiss is tentative, probing. Apologetic. My shoulders relax, unwinding from their coiled state.

"It was an ill-spoken attempt at humor and you are tired. Go and rest. You may dream of me."

The next kiss is quick and playful.

He speaks a series of now-familiar words before I can answer his flirtations. I'm ripped away from his side and tossed back into my bedroom.

"Easily flustered," I mutter.

I've finished the devil dog and moved on to my third repair, the twisted, bulging demon face that helps drain water from the roof when it rains. A true gargoyle. Time and water have smoothed its features to a near-shapeless lump, and I'm determined to resuscitate it and give it new life.

I'm still annoyed at how Adriel finds amusement at dumping me back into a deep sleep in my bed with little to no warning. And I am not at all flustered about the way he let me know exactly what kind of work I have ahead in the coming nights, once I've freed his right leg from its stone prison.

"You and your ridiculous penis!" I yell out, knowing he can hear me fine from his northern perch without all the extra volume.

Cock, Lauren. I can practically hear his voice, rich with humor, murmuring in my ear. *You can't even say it.*

"Prick." I pause. "Dickhead."

I shake out my hands, willing the irritation from my fingers. I can't afford to let my agitated state affect the next steps of this project. It wouldn't do to chisel off the fangs that I carved out this morning.

"See? I can say things *just fine*. I am not that easily flustered!"

Maybe it's time for a lunch break.

I hop from my little platform to the roof's edge and pull myself over the side. After brushing all the fine dust off my coveralls, I head down the ridiculous amount of stairs to the ridiculous kitchen of this ridiculous manor, looking for the ridiculous Cook that I am supposed to be avoiding, and who I suspect avoids me, too.

Not finding her, I make myself two sandwiches, grab a banana, and stomp my way back up to the roof with my meal.

I don't want to think about Adriel while I eat, or the flutter in my chest when he said he wouldn't look at other women. But lunch alone doesn't require much brain power, so I find myself reflecting back on last night's conversation.

And the kissing.

"I am not even going to miss you tonight," I say for Adriel's benefit. "I'm going to get a full night's sleep, and maybe even have a hot dream while I'm at it. A *real* dream."

Maybe one where I'm not being toyed with by an annoying wannabe manticore who gets his kicks by winding me up so he can send me away at his convenience, instead of finishing what he started and bringing me to a mind-blowing orgasm again.

"Not that I wanted you to do that. Because I am still off-limits, got it?"

Big talk there, Lauren. I brush bread crumbs off my hands. *Shut up, self. You're a pain in your own ass.*

With nothing to do at the end of the work day, I dig out the McGregor book I borrowed from manor's library and settle in to read the chapter on Kinloch.

The first pages contain a rather dry history of the manor, noting how unusual it was to find a fortified tower of this style in this region of Scotland. The original tower had been expanded into the manor house that exists today, and is considered one of the most well-preserved examples of late medieval period fortifications.

In a flash, I'm annoyed I can't question Adriel tonight about the manor, and why he claims to be older than the actual building. I make a mental note to ask him tomorrow night.

I've avoided thinking about Adriel's claims. Accepting something very strange is afoot at Kinloch is one thing; accepting that Adriel is a seven hundred-plus year old mage, that's next level shit.

My confused frustration leads me to a memory of advice my dad used to give me. The first time he said it, I was twelve, shaping little animal figures from clay at my worktable. He announced we would be moving again, and I'd smashed the bear I'd spent the last two hours sculpting.

Don't be caught out by what life hands you, Lauren. Shape it into the right form, just like you do that clay. It became his favorite saying. As a teenager, it annoyed me. But after my parents died, I embraced it and learned to roll with the punches in life.

To shape it into what I wanted it to be, something I've been doing on my own for a long time now. I believe it's a lesson I can apply at Kinloch.

On the next page, there's a portrait of one of the McCardle ancestors. I hold it up to catch more light across the page. I think it looks like the same portrait hanging on the wall in the main entrance. It is a remarkable likeness of the current Lord McCardle and I try not to consider how many cousins had to marry to make that happen.

I ignore Adriel's claims that my Lord McCardle is the same person he calls Cardle, his magic-wielding rival.

The sketches of the manor's statues capture the personalities of the stone in ways photographs cannot. I closely examine all the drawings, lingering over those of Selene and Adriel.

Were they in love? Before they were stone?

I shake my head, dismissing the attempt of my brain to go down that route. Turning the pages, I devour the facts presented before moving to the 'local legends' section.

...rumours have long existed about Kinloch Manor. Villagers in nearby Kinloch Leath report hearing strange cries in the forest, which many in the village liken to that of a lion's roar...

...past overnight visitors have told tales of unexplained sounds and dark shadows caught from the corner of the eye...

...feelings of being watched...

...close-mouthed on the family history, which village gossips whisper about at the local pub until shushed by...

"Well, the McCardles are cursed now, aren't they? Unlucky all around, but they've managed to keep the estate in the family all these years." The village elder shakes his head. He insists on anonymity, fearful of the family's retribution. "That Lord and his father before him, well, they're gruff fellas who don't like being spoken of. And dire lookin' to boot. Sure, and the wives don't seem to fare well marryin' into that family."

There's more than a little talk of mysterious disappearances, sudden illnesses, madness, and a spouse that may have run off with the gardener, or the butler, depending on who you talk to.

The current staff is small, but loyal, and this author is unable to find any sources of news from that quarter. Requests to stay at the manor overnight were denied by the current Lord McCardle.

I do some math. Maybe the author means McCardle's grandfather or even great-grandfather refused him access to Kinloch.

I reposition myself and yawn, stretching out across my bed. Flipping a page, I spare a passing thought that Adriel was right to give me the night off. Spending the days on the walls and the nights on the roof, helping Adriel out of his rocky shell, have drained me.

Well, I don't miss him. Not even a little. I'm glad to have the time to myself so I can catch up on my reading.

I wonder how he'll pass the night.

"I'm sure you can entertain yourself," I say, in case he has an ear out. "According to you, you've been at it for centuries."

Silence.

Blowing air between my lips, I flop onto my back and stare at the ceiling. I close my eyes and force my muscles to relax, breathing in and out slowly. I wait for the sensation of being yanked into Adriel's space, but it doesn't come. One eye squints open, but nothing has changed.

Twenty impatient minutes later, I'm still in my own bed, glaring at the ceiling and thinking about an ungrateful lion-shaped man. Does he even still count as a manticore? He spends more hours as a stone lion by day than he does in his revived man-form. Which isn't even finished, but could be if he would let me work.

Work.

I reach for my laptop and open the files for this contract so I can compare the photos to the sketches in the book. Only minor damage is noticeable in the drawings, and I have to wonder if the artist minimized it on purpose, or if it simply wasn't there at the time the writer visited.

Maybe the wild thunderstorm that blew Selene to smithereens caused the additional damage that prompted McCardle to call me in.

It's unusual for me to look at statuary and do anything but marvel. The chance to work on such unique pieces helped draw me to Kinloch. Yet the longer I look at the drawings, the more unsettled I feel.

The east wall contains a figure I've never seen duplicated anywhere else. A human face, locked in a rictus of pain and horror. Four snakes sprout from the stone surrounding the face. Two strike the face, fangs sunk deep into the cheeks. The other two are coiled, one above, and one below, offering a threat to any who approach.

Strange dreams lead to restless sleep, and threaten to blow away like dandelion fluff in the wind when I try to grab onto them. Adriel whispers lyrical words in my ear, disappearing into shadow when I turn to him. McCardle tells me I won't get my next payment unless I return Adriel to stone.

"You're threatening the order of the universe," he says.

Cook won't let me outside because all the silver spoons are missing. She threatens to call Scotland Yard.

"That's not actually in Scotland," I say, and she yells incomprehensible words that make my ears ring.

My alarm blares. It's going to be a long work day.

When I free Adriel's right leg the next night, his head drops into his hands and he grows so still and silent I'm afraid he might have turned back to stone.

"Adriel?" I whisper, and run careful fingers through his ink-black locks. His hair spills down over his shoulders, an untamed mass, less like a mane now and more like a human in need of a haircut. I use my fingers to massage his scalp and neck.

"Rest," he rumbles, and I'm given no choice but to go.

Adriel

Three nights until the full moon. Lauren has only been at Kinloch for a short while, but my heart is sure I have always known her.

"That is not possible," I tell my stone heart, but it ignores me.

Just like my cock didn't listen long ago when I told it bedding Selene, Cardle's wife, was a bad idea.

Nothing I've garnered from her tales gives a clue why or where Lauren gained her magic. A glimmer of an idea took shape when she said she was adopted as an infant, but she knows nothing about her birth parents. Since she has done nothing else we could identify as magic, the thought did not lead anywhere.

On stiff legs, still gray as stone, I pace the rooftop. Tomorrow night, Lauren will run her hands over me and restore them to full flesh. And she will no longer be able to ignore the one part of me she avoids at all costs.

Perhaps. But not if you say something else colossally stupid and drive her away, animal.

If Cardle marshalled an army of women to Kinloch, Lauren's presence would eclipse them all. When she exposed that rare flash of vulnerability, why could I not say those words and then speak of her charms, like the tilt of her head when she is deep in thought? Instead I played predator and latched onto her throat with my verbal claws, ready to tear it out.

I have been trapped in cold stone for too long.

And she asked me again about my chest, but I managed to delay her curious touch there. Lauren's magic is beyond my own experiences, and I am loath to admit to her that I don't know what will happen when my heart transforms.

In the room below, Lauren wonders aloud if she might be losing her mind, but she doesn't fool me. She wants to provoke me into bringing her across the Veil, but I need her to be at her best tomorrow night. Such an impatient creature, my blossom, but she hasn't had my lengthy practice at waiting.

If I ignore the one slip, my diplomacy skills *have* grown. I did not tell Lauren that she should have patience, and that of course I know what's best for us both.

See? I can learn.

But it might be amusing to see the flash of outrage in her eyes, and feel the sting of her barbed tongue flaying me should I say it within her hearing. Lauren keeps the nights alive with possibilities and lights up the mundane routine of my existence with her fire.

Spreading out her visits this past sennight borders on torture. I've always preferred the role of lover over fighter. Torture is best left to battle chiefs and witches.

Lauren's beauty consumes my thoughts tonight, distracting me from the changes she crafts on my form. It's not her clothing. She's opted for her favorite "comfy clothes" and her hair is up again.

Except for that one tendril she keeps pushing behind her ear. It's not long before it breaks loose and brushes her cheek. She tucks it back once more and stands examining me with her hands on her hips.

"All right," she says, her tone brisk and full of command. She might have trained warriors in her past life. "Stand up and turn around."

She's worked on both my legs, changing the gray veneer into a sun-kissed brown, bringing sensation screaming back into the nerves. I wiggle my toes anytime I doubt the reality of the change.

I offer her my back, and she chokes on laughter.

"Something amuses?"

"Just the idea that I'm about to give you a butt massage, and that's a phrase I don't say much. Or maybe ever."

I glance over one shoulder and take in the way she worries her bottom lip with her teeth. Does the woman even know how much temptation she offers by simply existing?

"Well. Here we go," she says, and puts her magic to work on my buttocks.

It's not my fault they're still gray, but Lauren acts as if I conspired to make it so in order to have her hands on them.

"Stop making that moaning noise." She snaps out the command, her hands smoothing themselves over flesh, up, down, up, down.

"It's how I say thank you," I say, glad she cannot see my smile at this moment.

My smile turns to a delighted laugh when she smacks me lightly on the backside to announce she's finished. Her fingertips trail over my living flesh, and a delicious shiver runs up my spine.

"How can you be so warm and breathe if your heart isn't beating?" Her fingers trace the knobs of bone in my spine, moving up, chasing the sensation she created.

"How can you change stone to flesh when you don't know how your magic works?" The words sound harsher than I intended, and her touch turns hesitant. "Give me your hands." She slips her arms around my waist from behind.

I flatten her hands against my stomach and place mine over the top of hers to guide her touch. I avoid my chest, but let her wield her power over my lower abdomen until I'm freed.

She leans into me, and I savor the warmth of her body, the soft swell of her breasts pressed against my back, the rise and fall of her erratic breathing.

So, I'm not the only one affected by this closeness.

It's good not to be alone.

"Lauren." I lift her hands so I can kiss each of her fingertips. I sense the power thrumming beneath the skin and know she's not done for the night. My smile curls against her fingers, and she uses her forefinger to trace my lips. I nip the end of her finger.

"It's time for the last of it." I release her and stay still, letting her take time to adjust to her next task.

"Are you ready?" she says, her voice cracking.

"As you can well see, I am always ready."

She blows a huff of faux outrage, and it brushes over my skin, raising gooseflesh. Lauren moves, taking her warmth but coming to face me, a mere arm's length away. Tonight she's bold, looking deep into my eyes with her moss-green ones. It's no accident that the soft forest bed I create here matches that color.

"All right," she whispers, and reaches for the unwieldy stone shaft. Just before she touches me, she jerks her hands back. "What if...what if I, uh...what if the stone b-breaks. Off. Completely."

I throw back my head and roar laughter.

"It's not funny, Adriel!" Lauren's cheeks burn bright red, but her eyes hold a glint of defiance. "Are you sure?" Her tongue darts out, wetting dry lips.

"Have *any* of my limbs fallen off under your care?" I swallow more amusement, feeling lighter in said limbs.

"Smart ass. Don't blame me if your dick drops off." She glares at me, hands on her hips. "Stop smiling at me like that." Her glance falls to my waist. "It makes it har—difficult to concentrate."

I fold my lips inward and bite down to get my smile under control. If it weren't for this protrusion, I would sweep Lauren into my arms and distract her from the task at hand.

"Continue."

She reaches for me, and grasps the end of the stone phallus. Her fingers can't fully wrap around the girth, and her shocked expression almost frees my laughter again.

Lauren's power surges into the base of my spine, and I choke back a gasp. Her other hand joins the first. The stony tip crumbles away within seconds.

Lauren jumps back with a startled yelp. "Oh my god, are you hurt?"

"If you wish to worship me, Lauren, I will not try to dissuade you." Before she can reply, I've taken her hands and wrapped them around the last impediment to my freedom. "I am not hurt." I stroke our hands up and down, feeling that tingle in my spine once more. "Tell me the length of this in your American measures."

"Tw-twenty inches," Lauren whispers. She meets my gaze.

I continue my distraction. "That sounds quite impressive." I lift an eyebrow, preening for her.

"Were you born this arrogant, or have you been practicing?"

I lean down and let my lips rest on the shell of her ear. "What you see before you is all I was born with. Look for yourself if you wish."

She jerks her head back. Her pupils flare wide open and she focuses on her hands. Everything I most definitely was *not* born with has crumbled away to fine dust. All that's left is *me*. I lift her right hand and hold it against my cheek.

"Keep going, Lauren."

The power rushes through her and into my flesh. She doesn't need my prompting, so I loosen my grip. Her right hand stays in motion, stroking the gray skin of my cock.

The change happens so fast that both of us are caught off guard. Lightning sears me, blurring my vision and threatening to drive me to my knees.

The words I utter come out in my native tongue, slurred. Lauren pauses, and squeezes the rigid, living flesh in her hand. No longer stone, but still hard. I don't know what I expected, seeing as Cardle cursed me when I was mid-thrust in his wife, but it surprises me to find myself still aroused. My eyes slip closed and I shift my hand to her hip, letting her continue on her own.

It's been so very long.

She resumes her strokes, changing her touch from the way she handles stone to the gentle care she has always taken with my true flesh. I'm drowning, every nerve in my body singing Lauren's name. The long-delayed release denied centuries ago brews inside of me.

Her touch is light, considerate of my dry skin, but I can't stop a deep moan from passing my lips. Lauren pauses. "No, don't stop now."

Lauren lets out a shaky breath. "I guess I owe you one," she says, humor lacing her voice. Her thumb strokes my cheek in the same slow, steady rhythm her other hand strokes my cock.

My fingers dig into her hip, and another small noise escapes me. A deep ache starts in my balls, and I gasp out her name.

Lauren's lips brush my neck, then move along my jawline. I tip my head down and capture her mouth with my own. Drawing a deep breath through my nose, I inhale the clean scent of her skin, and slide my tongue between her silken lips, probing. She sighs, and drops her hand down to cup my balls, squeezing lightly.

A low growl slips from my mouth and into hers. Her hand trails up the base of my cock and circles the head, driving me closer to the precipice. My hips rock of their own accord, following the rhythm she sets for my body.

And then the reality sets in.

I'm finally free of my stone form in the Veil now, and it's all due to this woman, the one whose hand works one final feat of magic upon me.

"Lauren, I—"

That's all the warning either of us get.

My orgasm comes roaring up from the depths of my being. A primal cry tears from my throat. My cock pulses, and my release erupts with the ferocity of a volcano.

Lauren shrieks and begins babbling. "Adriel! Oh my god, are you all right? Oh shit!" She's staring at her hands, and in torch light, it appears her hands are covered with a thousand tiny stars.

I drop to my knees, shuddering, weak with relief. Eyes blurred with tears, my fingers grope and find a thin line of granite dust at my feet.

Lauren is on her knees facing me, running her hands over my shoulders, my arms, still babbling hysterically about damaging me. I catch her hands, and examine them.

"Stop it, Lauren! Stop!" I pull her into my arms, and lean back, cradling her against me.

I calm her enough to make her understand that my first blinding orgasm in centuries consisted of nothing but debris. The same dust that's fallen at Lauren's feet after she dissolved the wings on my back, the stone encasing my body, and the extended length of my stone erection.

After examining the dust on her hands, I rock us back and forth with my laughter.

Lauren

"I t's not funny, you big asshole!" I shout and embarrass myself further by bursting into noisy sobs against Adriel's shoulder.

"Oh, blossom, no crying. Come now, no need to mourn my cock. I assure you it is still attached. Everything will be fine." He strokes my hair, soothing me like I'm a small child having a fit.

I shove my hands between my knees to hide the way they're shaking. Flakes of mica glitter in the moonlight. When Adriel transformed from stone to warm human flesh—silk over steel—I should have released him. But the feel of him, the burning heat in his gaze and the heady scent of arousal in the air, all combined to cloud my thoughts and turn them in one direction. The dampness between my legs brings my attention to the empty ache there.

At the moment his orgasm was imminent, the words he'd said a few nights ago rang in my head, "*I remain uncertain what might happen should my heart begin beating again. I may well turn to dust and crumble away.*"

And when I was left with a hand covered in granite dust instead of the milky fluid I would have expected...

"Why did that happen?"

Adriel shrugs. "I have been entrapped in stone. Is it such a surprise?"

I lean back and stare into his eyes.

"Do you really believe you'll turn to dust if I finish?" I glance at his chest, the one patch of stone he has yet to ask me to free.

"I cannot say what will happen to me, love. But would it really be so bad?" His gaze slides away from mine, and the wistfulness in his voice sends a fissure of alarm along my nerves.

"Adriel! You'd die."

"And I have been alive, yet not lived, for centuries now." He rises, and sets me on my feet. "Observe."

And with that, he bolts across the roof and swan dives off the edge.

"*ADRIEL!*" I run to the spot where he disappeared from view, heart hammering and blood running ice cold in my veins.

Even with the bright moon, the darkness lays a thick blanket over Kinloch. I experience a flash of gratitude that I can't see his broken body on the cobblestones below.

"Get away from the edge, Lauren," Adriel says from behind me.

I jump and utter a surprised shriek.

"I will not be harmed, but if you fall, you will die both here and in the daylight world. You would not be the first in the Veil to meet a bad end on this roof."

"You bastard!" I fly at him, ready to slap his face for the scare he gave me. He catches both of my hands and spins me, crossing my arms and tucking me into a tight hold, my back against his chest.

I struggle against him, but it's pointless. As a lion, Adriel had been a massive figure, and as a man, he continues to loom large, towering over me and restraining me without effort.

"I am sorry. You were not to know I have jumped from this roof some two hundred times or more."

Shocked, my struggle against the iron of his arms stops. "What?"

"I cannot die in the Veil, Lauren," he says. "You, however, are vulnerable. Cardle stranded two of his mortal children here some three hundred years back, and they both threw themselves from the towers when they grew desperate enough. They were not part of the Veil."

"The Veil?" I ask numbly.

"This is the Veil."

"Why would you throw yourself from the tower over two hundred times?" I whisper, horrified into stillness.

Adriel strokes my hair, and presses his lips to my ear to whisper back. "Even the moon and night dwellers are not much in the way of company after so many centuries, my blossom. It is not an existence that can continue indefinitely if one wishes to retain one's sanity."

Maybe I should be afraid of him, but his words shatter my heart instead.

"McCardle's sons." I swallow the lump in my throat. "Could you have helped them?"

He exhales, ruffling my hair.

"Perhaps," he says at last. "I was not at my best in those years." His arm tightens around me and his voice changes to a low snarl. "But why should I help the progeny of my enemy? He would have only sent them back, or worse. One of his children resides on the east wall and has for some four hundred years. Another is on the west wall."

I need a distraction from the atrocity of these actions. And that Adriel could not, or would not, help them.

"McCardle is the man you call Cardle." I don't ask. He's dropped hints before, spoken poorly of the lord of the manor, and left me to wonder about the mysteries of Kinloch and its past. Now is the time to push for more answers. "And he's as old as you?"

"A bit older. I am uncertain of how he spent his years before we met. And we do not have occasion, or the desire, to exchange histories."

He releases me without warning, and prowls around the perimeter of the roof. I set off after him, afraid he'll jump again.

Not that it would matter, I guess.

"Tell me how you became trapped here."

He tips his head back, the muscles in his neck straining. Both palms slap the top of the low wall, and his chest heaves. I rest my hand on his forearm, offering what comfort I can, and he covers it with one of his own.

We fall into silence.

I peer at him from the corner of my eye and allow myself an appreciation of his profile. Until tonight, I'd been able to distract myself from his handsome face. Encased as he was in stone, it had been easy to ignore his appeal, or to simply admire him as art.

Now I have time to study him, and let my mind wander to how it felt to be trapped against his body. Whoever he was in his other life, Adriel was no couch potato. Everything about him is solid, imposing. In modern times, his physique would rival that of an Olympic athlete, sculpted perfection on every level.

"I will try to tell you of how Selene came to be cursed," he says, breaking the silence and interrupting my musings on his compelling beauty.

He's talking about serious things and you're thinking about how delicious he looks fully human. Even my own brain sounds disgusted with me.

"It is not a tale I wish to revisit. There is nothing in any of it that is noble or ends happily or...whatever people love stories to be." He leans over the parapet, eyes scanning the ground like he's looking for a better spot to try his jump again. He whispers, almost inaudible. "And you will know what manner of man you have resurrected."

Adriel continues, "Selene was young when she was joined to Cardle. Her clan offered her to broker peace. And so the young girl was given to the older head of a rival clan. It was hate at first sight."

"They were, by all reports, never pleased with one another. He complained she could give him no living sons, and she complained that he was a poor provider and cold-hearted."

"Were you part of his clan? Cardle's?"

"Nay. I was—" He pauses. "But this is a story about Selene. It can only be told that way."

I bite my tongue on further questions, so he can tell the story.

"Several years into a most unhappy arrangement, a traveling mage entered the clan's territory." Adriel turns his head far enough for me to see his sardonic smile. "I'm told he was quite handsome and charming. So much so that the young wife of the headman became enamored of him."

"So she seduced y-, uh, the mage." *I do* not *feel jealous*, I repeat several times.

"Admittedly, it did not take much effort. Our man was a bit of a *pachaich* in those days."

My mind translates this unknown phrase to *manwhore*.

"Why did he come to stay with Cardle's clan?"

Adriel's expression turns grim, and he shrugs one shoulder.

"His mage's apprenticeship was done, his warrior's training completed. And his own clan had been decimated by yet another war, followed by a disease that further ravaged their numbers." He gazes toward the forest. "Those numbers included his own wife and child."

Tears sting my eyes. He slips his arm around my waist, but keeps his face turned away.

"Adriel..." I don't know what else to say.

"It was long ago. And that marriage had also been dictated by clan allegiances. That was not unusual in those days." He exhales a shaky breath. "Events happened so long ago, it is as if they happened to someone else."

"And so, the mage stayed with Cardle and his clan for a measure of time," he continues. "Cardle himself was a mage, but he practiced darker arts than that of his visitor. The foolish mage took up with the dark sorcerer's wife, who whispered in his ear that they should run away together."

I don't want to ask, but the words spill from my lips anyway. "Did you, I mean, he, love Selene?"

"No, blossom. Selene was a dalliance. And she did not love him either. They used each other in a time when they were both unhappy and searching. It was only their misfortune that Cardle discovered them together on the eve of the man's departure. Our mage had planned to move on the next day."

"What did Cardle do?"

"He imprisoned their souls. And later, he transformed them into stone monsters and displayed the trophies along the walls of his keep."

"Are Selene and the others able to come out at all? Like you?"

Adriel shakes his head. "No magic in them."

"What happened to Selene's soul when lightning struck her stonework?"

"I believe I felt her soul depart this world."

He turns his ravaged expression on me and I catch my breath at the glint of sorrow and madness in his slate eyes. I cup his face in my hands and brush my lips over his.

Adriel's thumb swipes across my cheek and he licks my tears from his skin. "Go to bed, Lauren. Come to me at the full moon."

"Don't—"

But it's too late. Adriel sends me into a deep, dreamless sleep with a string of words.

I spend much of the next two working days vacillating between anger and sadness so often I'm dizzy from it. I'll tell Adriel if he pulls any-more suicidal stunts, I won't return.

And if McCardle shows up, I don't know if I can keep my temper and not slap him across the face.

You know you sound like you've gone insane. You believe you spend your nights on the roof with a centuries-old mage, and that the man who hired you is the one who trapped that mage's soul in a grotesque.

Life is weird. And yet, I don't think I've gone crazy. It would be so much easier if I had.

The full moon arrives.

After dinner, I prepare a surprise for Adriel and slip upstairs to my bed.

I've never tried carrying something with me, though I crossed back with the moss and pebble, so I think this will work. I hope so; we should celebrate his freedom from the stone.

With a tight grip on my gift, I concentrate, trying my best to block out distracting thoughts. I want to get to Adriel as soon as possible, and it's hard to dampen my nervous excitement enough so I can cross over. I'm uncertain what his mood will be after the revelations of two nights ago.

"Lauren!" A smile splits Adriel's face, and he rushes toward me from the far side of the roof.

I'm relieved his excitement matches mine, and I smile back.

I set the bowl on the bench just in time. He swings me up and into the air, spinning us around twice. My laughter rings across the rooftop.

"Put me down before I get sick."

He brings me close, and lowers me slowly. I slither down the front of his rock-hard *human* body and it sinks in that Adriel is completely naked.

"Don't you have any clothes?"

His brow creases. "Why would I waste power conjuring clothing?"

"Because..."

Other than saying, *I might not be able to keep my eyes to myself*, I can't really think of a legitimate reason. "Never mind. I brought you something."

I lift the bowl and present it to him.

"Lauren," he says in a hushed tone. "Is that...is it ice cream?"

"Rum and raisin," I say. His eyes gleam, and my smile threatens to crack my face.

He takes the bowl with both hands, handling it with the reverence belonging to a sacred object. I sit on the bench, and he joins me, our bodies angled toward each other. My right knee touches his left.

He occupied more physical space in his lion's form, but somehow he fills the bench with his presence like he's grown twice in size since I freed him.

"Better eat it before it melts."

Adriel grips the spoon in his fist and shovels the first bite into his open mouth. A passionate moan vibrates from his throat. He slides the spoon from between his closed lips, eyes rolling upward. I snort-laugh at the expression, but he ignores me. He scoops heaps of ice cream into his mouth at a frantic pace.

"Slow down, you're going—"

Adriel grunts in alarm, drops the spoon, and slaps his forehead with one hand.

"—to get brain freeze."

"What trickery is this?"

"Put your tongue on the roof of your mouth and press it there, then rub it around a bit," I say, offering sage advice I gained from my mother.

He gives me an incredulous look, but obeys. The creases in his forehead relax, and I bite back laughter. I lean over and pick up the spoon, handing it back with a cheeky grin. He resumes eating with a comical amount of caution.

Adriel licks every molecule of ice cream off the spoon with a slow precision that threatens my sanity.

He's scraping the bowl to get the melted goop and the last little hill of ice cream corralled onto the spoon when his head jerks up. His eyes are shining fever-bright.

"Lauren," he says, his voice a sensual caress.

He offers me the last precious bite of his treat.

My lips part of their own accord, and the spoon slips between them. I close my mouth around the cold metal and he withdraws it slowly, leaving the sweetness to rest on my tongue.

The naked hunger in his eyes is enough to melt a whole freezer full of ice cream.

"Thanks," I say, and almost cringe at how breathless I sound.

"It's a wonderful night." He sets the bowl under the bench. "The first night of the full moon. The ninth personal meeting between us. Three, three times over. It's a powerful portent."

His eyes narrow and I look down to see a fat drop of ice cream sliding down the inside of my thigh. He catches the dripping mess on his forefinger and drags the digit up, collecting more, leaving a sticky smear behind.

"Rum and raisin," he murmurs, and licks the melted goo from his finger while he pins me to the bench with the force of his stare.

I catch fire. I'm going to burn alive from the inside out and leave nothing but ash behind. The heat spreads from my belly, and my clit throbs in time with my heartbeat. I shift, my once loose clothing too tight.

Adriel touches the corner of my mouth with the finger he just licked, and trails it lightly over my bottom lip.

"Do you still taste of it?"

"It?" I'm sure the blood flow has left my brain and traveled directly south, or I would know what he was saying.

He licks his lips. "I wondered if anything could make you even more of a temptation to me. And now I believe the answer is yes." Adriel dips his head, slanting his mouth over mine. This is no mere sampling. He consumes my lips with intent, nibbling, licking, probing. I open my mouth to him, and our tongues tangle in a wild dance.

Adriel pulls me onto his lap so that I'm straddling him, knees next to his hips. I cling to his neck and shoulders. One hand plunges into my hair, holding me in place, and the other finds its way beneath my shirt. He slides his large hand up over my stomach, slowly, at odds with the frantic clashing of our tongues.

When his hand closes over my breast, I moan against his lips, and press restlessly against his questing fingers. He breaks the kiss, regarding me through half-lidded eyes.

"I would make you mine tonight, Lauren. Do you accept me freely?"

"Yes."

Gentle fingers find my nipple, and he pinches it between his thumb and forefinger. Lightning travels into the valley between my legs and I trap a whimper in my throat. Adriel's lips shift into a sly smile, and he repeats the maneuver until he's worked my nipple into a stiff peak.

His cock twitches against my thigh, held captive beneath me. I reach down, and shifting slightly, take his growing member in hand, moving him so that his erection is pressed between our bodies.

"*Fyxe*." He whispers the word, and even though I don't know its meaning, the way he says it causes heat to pool between my thighs.

He moves his hand to my other breast. "Lift your arms."

I obey, and he slips my t-shirt off and tosses it aside. He grasps my neck, one arm wrapped around my waist.

"Hang on to my arms, and relax," he says, and he leans me backwards. His palm splays against the center of my back, supporting me. I grip his forearms for support.

"I wish I could draw this out. I would make love to you under these stars until you cry to me for mercy." His hand dips between my legs and he slips two fingers up the loose leg of my shorts, brushing the backs of them against my soaking wet pussy.

"I can smell your arousal," he purrs, and presses a knuckle against my clit. "And you're so wet for me, I could feel it through this clothing." He slips one finger inside me, and twirls it gently.

"I'd prefer to spend even more time sipping nectar from this lovely flower." He slips a second finger in and works them in and out, his movement steady, firm. "But I have waited for you for too many centuries to hold back anymore."

I'm squirming against his fingers and working to keep my over-stimulated body from betraying me too soon.

"Tell me what you want," he says, and circles his thumb over my clit.

"I want you inside me, Adriel. Now."

Adriel

As much as I want to savor her, I slip my fingers from Lauren's slick hole, and shove the fabric of her shorts aside. She lifts herself with her knees, grasping me in one hand and setting the other on my shoulder.

Lauren and I look deep into each other's eyes. Can she see my soul in the same way hers shines for me?

Eyes glowing with desire, she rubs the engorged head of my cock against her opening, mingling our juices.

"You're so big," she says.

I should reassure her, but she smiles and licks her lips. My member swells in response. It's all I can do not to throw her down on the bench and slake my hunger.

"Take your pleasure of me." I offer myself instead, resisting the urge to grab her hips and slam her down onto my raging erection. Enthralled by the sight of her tongue darting out to lick her lips again, my lust surges. "Tease me no more, blossom. I'm as ready to blow as a young lad with his first woman."

Her eyes clear for a moment, and she says, "Adriel, about the other night. About the...the dust when I...when you. When you came."

My beautiful shy blossom.

"It won't happen again," I say, torn between my desire to laugh and my desire to mate.

Lauren bites her bottom lip and sinks slowly onto my straining cock. So slowly it might be considered torture. My eyes roll up as her heat envelops me fully. She's so tight around me.

She moans, a sound that travels straight to my sword sheathed inside her. I go still, letting her adjust to the way I fill her. I kiss her, probing and withdrawing in a steady rhythm.

I want to continue touching and teasing her, but I surrender to my need. One hand keeping her clothing out of the way, I spread the other across the base of her spine. I breathe in, count to ten. My control hangs by a thread.

She rolls her hips, and I purr deep in my throat. Lauren flexes her legs and rises slowly, lifting herself until only the head of my cock remains inside her.

I flick my tongue over a rosy nipple and kiss the stiff tip before sucking it into my mouth. Her passion is as rampant as my own, and I can't hold back.

I grab her hips and pull her down. She grinds against me again and again. Our rhythm seeks pure gratification, its only desire to quench our bodies' thirst. The universe could not have sent a better woman to suit me; she wants her pleasure as much as I, and rides me in a ruthless search for it.

Her rough breathing spikes my lust. I sense she's close, and I am barely held in check at the thought, lifting and dropping her onto my rock-hard cock. She's dripping, soaking my balls, and the wet sounds of our arousal fills my ears.

The moon witnesses our joining, painting Lauren's skin alabaster in its glow. Energy thrums through me. I could take on a band of warriors and their mages all alone with the power I've absorbed.

"Oh, Adriel, you feel so good, I can't...I need to..." Lauren says, her voice urgent, breathless. "I'm coming."

"Yes." I groan. "That's it, blossom. Let me have it." Limited by my position, I rock my hips into her at every downstroke.

She gives an abrupt cry, and convulses in my arms, clenching around my cock. Her head tips back, her lips parted so her soft cries can escape.

One hand on her shoulder, one on her hip, I slam her down onto my cock and it swells and pulses, my seed pumping into her. Grabbing a fist full of her hair, I bring my mouth to hers and suck her soft whimpers into my mouth, savoring the way her quivering walls milk me of every drop.

We're panting against each other's mouths, and I gentle the kiss.

"My little flower." My cock is half-hard, still showing interest in all the things I want to do with her.

I shift Lauren, and smile at her disappointed moue when my cock slips from her. Setting her on her feet and kneeling, I tug her loose fitting shorts down and off, and use them to wipe between her legs, tidying the mess I've made of her.

Guilt pierces me when I see that the stone bench scraped her knees and shins. I swing her up into my arms and carry her to the elevated moss bed I summon into being with a mere thought. It is the least I can offer after her generosity to me.

If I had not been in such a rush, she would not have come to harm. *You did not even have the patience to undress her first, did you, beast?* Perhaps I am still more monster than man.

"What are you thinking?" she asks, cupping my cheek with her palm. "You look angry."

"With myself. You are hurt."

"Hurt?" She frowns.

I set her on the edge of the bed, and kneel again. Whispering words of renewal, I brush my lips over her scraped skin. The power that has flowed between us tonight, near the height of the full moon, is more than enough to aid a small healing.

"Oooohh," Lauren says, her eyes rounded in astonishment. The skin is smooth, unblemished.

She turns her bright smile to me, and if it is the last thing I see in any of the worlds, it will be enough.

"You look so serious," she says. She swallows hard. "Do you have regrets?"

"I have many regrets." I answer in truth. "But you will never be one of them."

Her expression warms, and I kiss the inside of one knee. Time to distract her before she continues probing.

"How did you know? About the dust, I mean. That when you, uh, that it wouldn't happen again?"

I chuckle. She never fails to amuse, and these questions are safer ground.

"How do you think I spent last night, my first full night of freedom? I ran the perimeter of the castle roof for some time, and later I took myself in hand and thought of you. More than once."

"Adriel!" But she laughs, and the sound rings like a bell across the rooftop.

I do not mention how I also prowled the halls and rooms of Kinloch, the ones from which I am not barred by runes. How I ended the night keeping watch over her sleep until the first fickle light of sunrise sent me back to my daytime prison. Lauren's presence helped control the discomfort of being indoors too long after centuries spent under the open sky.

"Freedom has a remarkable effect on a man." I kiss her knee again, then trail my lips upward, licking and nipping along her inner thigh. The muscles tighten then relax under my ministrations. Her toes flex, and I catch the scent of her musk, a sign she enjoys my attention.

"You're impossible," she says.

"I am very possible."

"And humble, as always." She's smiling down at me, and I wink.

"I owe you more than some rushed pairing on a hard bench."

"You don't *owe* me. And I was very much involved in that rushed pairing." Her hand smooths back a lock of hair from my forehead. "If you *are* a dream, you're the best one I've ever had."

I purr my agreement and take her left foot, rubbing it with both hands. Fingers digging gently into the muscles of her calf, I work my way upward. When I reach her thigh, I make sure my fingertips occasionally brush her sex as I massage her flesh.

"Lie on your stomach. Let me do for you as you have for me these past nights," I say, and help her reposition on the mossy bed.

Soft sighs of pleasure slip from Lauren's lips, her body relaxing under my care. Her questions have ceased, and I do not break the easy silence between us with speech. I let my wandering hands and delicate kisses on her skin speak my regard for her.

I'm hard again by the time my hands cup the sweet flesh of her backside. I knead each cheek with my fingers and she shifts under my hands. My tongue draws a lazy circle, and I suck flesh into my mouth. I bite down, careful not to break skin, and she gasps. I repeat the same treatment on the other cheek, running a fingertip over the mark I left behind on the first.

I kiss the base of her spine, and flatten my palms against her ass, squeezing. "Tease," she says, mock accusation evident in her voice.

"A promise I will deliver on," I say, and go to work on her back.

I trail my tongue up her spine and her skin pimples with gooseflesh. She shifts again, but I pin her into place so she can't move. I can't let her provoke me into haste; I need to savor her.

Time slows to a crawl.

I allow her to turn over, and massage her arms and precious fingers before I set my hands on her shoulders. She's watching me through half-lidded eyes, her body warm and inviting, and mine for the taking.

"You're looking very smug," she says.

The intent written on her face causes me to warn, "Keep your magical hands to yourself, woman, or I'll send you to your bed. Alone." Lauren has no way to suss out my empty threat, and tucks her hands at her sides with a sly smile.

I lavish attention on her breasts until she's panting and her nipples are hard peaks against my tongue.

She groans in frustration.

"Did you have a complaint, blossom?" The question sounds innocent, as intended, but she balls her hands into fists and exhales a shaky breath.

"No."

"Then spread your legs, and let me see how wet you are for me."

She makes a sound low in her throat, but does as she's told. In the moonlight, she glistens and I have to take a deep breath to calm my raging desire. I'm so hard I fear my cock may burst.

And still, I won't be rushed.

I kneel between her legs and spread her petals, admiring the beauty before me. With reverence, I sip her, using my tongue to lap up every drop.

Lauren comes to life, and I forget my toothless threats to send her to her bed. One hand grips my hair in a loose fist, the other fondles her breast. I can't let watching her distract me from my feast.

"Adriel." She moans, and I flick the button at the top of her opening with my tongue until she cries out again. The warm flood of her release fills my mouth and I drink eagerly until she stops quaking.

I kiss my way along her body, up to her mouth, and let her taste herself on my tongue.

The haze of pleasure mists her eyes, and my lust nearly gets the better of me. I slide my shaft along her opening, up and down, several times. The heat of her threatens to set me aflame.

"Tell me what you want of me, Lauren. Speak it into being." I hover over her, propped on my hands, careful to keep my stone chest from making contact.

"You," she says, simple and direct. Something else I admire about her.

I press the head of my cock forward, slowly, slowly, slipping into her with ease, both of us well-primed.

"This?"

"Yes."

Forward, forward, until I'm buried inside her and she wraps her legs around my waist, holding me deep. I grind against her and she whimpers in response and flexes her hips.

The moonlight reflects in her eyes, glinting with power. I withdraw until I've nearly pulled out, then allow myself to sink back into her molten depths.

"You feel so good," she whispers, stealing the words from me.

I rock into her over and over, holding back my feverish need. She meets my thrusts each time. I lean onto one elbow, and lace the fingers of my hand with hers, pinning her in place.

My pace quickens, and she responds to my hard, deep thrusts, matching me with equal passion.

"Are you close?"

"Yes." She doesn't beg, but I hear the plea in her one-word answer. "I wish you would kiss me."

"Not yet, blossom. Soon, I promise." The slapping of our flesh coming together echoes in the night, and Lauren's breathing catches. Her sweetness lingers on my tongue, and I wish I had time for a final taste, but it's best not to linger over-long now.

I grab her free hand, circling the wrist.

"I'm coming, Adriel," she says. "Don't stop. I want to come for you."

Her words are ambrosia; I drive into her with a steady rhythm, keeping my eyes on her face. Her lips part and she shouts something incoherent, her tight walls clamping around my manhood, rippling and pulsating with the strength of her climax.

"It's too much." She whimpers, but I don't let up.

I'm on the verge, ready. "I need you," I say. "Now, Lauren. *Now.*" I press her palm to my chest and trap it over the stony surface covering my heart.

The soft look of fulfillment slips from her face, and her eyes widen in alarm. She tugs on her hand, but can't escape my grasp.

"Yes." I groan, overcome in every sense. The buzzing in my ears drowns out everything. My skin prickles, tears clouding my vision, and I plough into Lauren with short, quick strokes.

Dust and pebbles run between her fingers, falling from my breast to hers. She struggles, but it's useless. I have her body trapped beneath mine, and her hand in an iron-grip. Lauren shouts my name, panicked.

My heart thunders to life at the same instant my orgasm rips through me, and I roar, my liquid essence pouring into Lauren. We're throbbing in time together; even our heartbeats pound out the same rhythm.

When I've spilled every drop into her, I collapse, trapping her beneath me while I try to gather my wits. Lauren's fists are beating at my shoulders and back, but I can't focus on that.

Why am I still here?

I mutter in amazement. "Not dead."

I might be crushing Lauren, so I prop myself up to take some of my weight off her.

"You son of a bitch!" She thumps my chest. "You tried to die, and you tried to do it while we...while we were *fucking*."

"That was no mere fucking," I say, offended at the insinuation.

Lauren blisters the air with a string of curses, angrier than when I jumped off the roof to demonstrate the oddities of my prison.

"I'm not dead."

"I'll throw you off this roof myself until you *do* die," she says between clenched teeth. Hot tears leak from her eyes.

"My love," I say, and kiss her.

She bites my lip hard enough to draw blood. But I cannot be hurt in the Veil. Not physically.

"How *could* you, Adriel? You told me you thought you might turn to dust and die if your heart beat again, and then you ambushed me and tried to kill yourself. Again! You fucking maniac!"

"How long until your work at the manor is complete?"

"What does that matter? We're talking about your latest suicide attempt!"

I repeat my question until I feel the anger drain from her in a rush. She cannot avoid my truth.

"You will finish the work and go home, Lauren. You cannot just stay on without reason, Cardle will not allow it, and you have a life to live. I will remain behind, alone." *Trapped in Cardle's stone prison.* "As a man, with only the memory of you to sustain me."

I gather her and roll so that we lay on our sides, facing each other.

"I had thought of waiting until your work was done. Of spending every night remaining to me in your company. And then I thought of trying to convince you to end me, and wondered if you would be able to do so. Or if I would be able to ask it of you." I wipe her tears. "You are tenderhearted, even when you are yelling at me."

"You'll be here forever?" she asks, her voice small. More tears fall.

I prefer the angry tears to these sorrowful ones.

"I do not know. It might well be for eternity. Or ten years, ten decades, ten centuries." *Or until Cardle's power crumbles at last. Who can say?*

"Oh, Adriel," she says, and the pity in her voice almost breaks me.

"Hush," I say, and pull her close. She trembles in my arms, contemplating my fate. Her tears are molten lava against my chest. I kiss the top of her head. "I am sorry, my blossom. I did not handle this well. It would perhaps have been best to discuss it first, but I feared you would never agree."

"You're right about that." She sniffles, and I rub her back. "Maybe." Her body presses itself tight against me. "I don't know if I could have left you trapped here forever. Or for however long." She puts her ear to my chest, listening to my heart beating.

"Think no more on it. Not tonight." I breathe her in, and relish the warmth of her against me. "I only wanted the joy of you, especially if it was to be my final night of existence."

"Kiss me again," she says.

Ever the obedient servant, I hasten to do her bidding.

Lauren

The forest path leads me deep into the woods, and the peace of it wraps itself around me, soothing irritations in my soul. I breathe the rich scent, a heady mixture of life blooming in early spring flowers and decay in the soil.

The forest has its own presence, almost as if another person walks beside me to keep me company in my search.

Adriel and I had a lot of back and forth about how he even knows the tree he wants me to find is out here, but I went looking at his insistence.

The rowan tree he described looms above me like a giant returned to earth from a myth, and I touch the rough bark.

All morning I've let uncertainty worm its way into my thoughts, questioning and doubting myself and my trust in Adriel.

What are you even doing here, Lauren?

With my hand on the ancient tree, the answer comes to me.

He's mine. I brought him from the stone lion's form, chiseled him out with my bare hands, and shaped him into the man he had once been. He is *mine*. That's why I believe in him, why I know he doesn't lie or play games with me. I've known since he settled at my side that first night that he belonged to me.

I set about gathering his requested items.

"Take a twig with a bud, and one with a flower. Then find the *daken* and peel—"

"Daken?"

His face had contorted in thought, and he waved a hand. "The daken. Your word is birch. And then the burrs from a burdock."

Adriel wants me to bring him all three, and a white ribbon to make a protection spell.

"And perhaps more ice cream would be useful," he'd said.

"What spell calls for ice cream?" I laughed at his hopeful expression, and kissed him goodnight. His attempt at looking stern in the face of my laughter failed, so he sent me to my bed.

Now if I can manage not to get lost on my way back.

It's impossible to concentrate on the work after I return from the forest. I decide to drive into the village and catch up on my emails and other overdue contacts. Maybe I'll buy Adriel some shorts of his own while I'm there. I'm curious what he'll make of wearing modern clothing. *If* he'll wear them. He seems perfectly at ease in his, uh, natural form.

And he mesmerizes me in that form. It'd be a shame to cover it up. *Let him decide.*

Time away from the manor gives me too much time to think. To wonder about the work I'm doing. I've avoided asking Adriel if I'm helping to keep the souls bound in their stone forms forever. If I'm somehow hurting them.

I don't need this job enough to keep these souls enchained.

"What happened to my rum and raisin?" Adriel asks when I hand him the chocolate ice cream. "It looks burnt. How did you burn something frozen?"

Laughter would be cruel, so I stuff a spoonful in my mouth and roll my eyes in delight. Adriel's nostrils flare and he cradles the bowl to his chest to protect it from my pilfering. Now it's safe to laugh, to tease him about his appetite for ice cream when he admits he feels no hunger.

"Not for food, at least." His eyes sparkle and my toes curl.

Chocolate ice cream inhaled, we move on to the shorts.

"You are remarkably prudish for a woman who wantonly gives herself to me for a mere spoonful of rum and raisin," he says, eyebrow cocked, smile roguish.

Still, he tries them on to please me, and expresses delighted curiosity over how much the pockets might hold.

"I want to spend the whole night up here," I say, interrupting his exploration. "With you."

His eyes search my face, quiet for so long I'm sure he's going to reject my request. Then he gives a brisk nod, and extends a hand. I offer the items I took from the forest earlier in the day.

"You need as much protection from *them* as I can provide." He gives me a sharp look. "You cannot let on that you know what Cardle has done, Lauren."

"Oh wow, thanks, Adriel. I planned to run out and accuse him the minute he shows up again."

He lifts his lip in a sneer. "You are a brat."

I fake a cough, bringing a fist to my mouth so I can hide my smile. *All growl, no bite.*

We settle on the mossy bed, sitting cross-legged and facing each other. Adriel lays the items out with care and traces a forefinger over each one. The longing in his face pains me to watch.

"What are you thinking?" I ask.

"That I miss the forest. It is a beautiful place, is it not?"

"It is," I agree.

He twirls the burdock. "You must stay still and silent while I complete the spellwork. I must concentrate, and it's important not to disrupt the incantation. The wrong movement, a misplaced word, an interruption, they all carry risk." One eyebrow cocks up, chastising me ahead of time not to interrupt with my inevitable questions.

Adriel braids the flexible twigs and burdock together carefully, and secures them in the birch bark I shaved from the tree. With whispered words, he wraps the bundle with an intricate set of knots before handing it over to me with further instructions.

"Tell me another story," I say, settling down and resting my head in his lap. I toy with the charm he gave me, earning a stern look. I tuck it into my pocket. "Tell me about the others. The other cursed ones."

Adriel

"Am I hurting them? Working on the stone?"

I stroke Lauren's hair, admiring the way the moonlight plays in the silky locks.

"No, blossom. They are beyond harm."

"But I'm making it possible for them to stay trapped here. Their souls. Would you like it, if you were stuck in the stone and didn't have your magic so you could come out?"

She doesn't add how much she needs this job to go well, and how much damage it would do her reputation if something goes wrong. But I have listened to her with more than my ears.

We stay up until the stars go to bed, taking turns telling stories, making love, and planning. I need Lauren to do something for me, something dangerous.

I need her to search Cardle's room.

The warding rune keeps me out, but Lauren can enter. He won't be expecting that since he didn't give her permission to mill about his manor. And Cardle can't imagine anyone doing anything he hasn't permitted.

Cook will be out. She has a routine that she rarely deviates from and will go to a town beyond little Kinloch Leath to do...whatever it is she does. Probably finding the bones of small children for her broth, or something equally nefarious. Her mother was worse, and her grandfather even more so. I suppose she can't help what she became under Cardle's influence.

From the wall, I extend my awareness. There's nothing I can do to protect Lauren when she conducts her search during daylight hours. I should have had her wait and gone with her tonight instead. I could have stood in the hallway, and directed her investigation. In my defense, I have not made battle plans in tandem in quite some time.

Lauren returns to her room empty-handed, a short time before Cook returns from gallivanting in town.

And then, just before sundown, Cardle arrives.

Perhaps I should have anticipated it. Likely Lauren tripped a hidden ward in his room even though she carried my talisman of protection.

"Oh! Lord C-McCardle," Lauren says, when he catches her taking ice cream from the freezer.

"The workmen are coming back in the morning to complete the setup on the roof. I thought I would stay the night and supervise. See how things are progressing."

"Oh," Lauren replies in a faint voice. She clears her throat. "I mean, that's great. I look forward to the work getting finished up." She drops the ice cream back in the freezer and winces when the top slams closed. "I-I spent a lot of time in the sun today, and didn't drink enough water. I think I'll go to bed early. Excuse me."

She flees.

Cardle looks after her thoughtfully, and I sense his interest in my blossom, a dastardly scratching that rakes against my thoughts.

I cannot allow her into the Veil, not while he's here. I'm forced to rebuff her, and it stings my heart. Even worse, it stings hers.

After she falls asleep, I manifest outside of Cardle's bedroom, a sentinel in the hallway. I linger in shadow and wait for him to come upstairs from the library.

He senses something, but he cannot see me where I stand. Tense in the shoulders, he enters his room, and before he takes more than three steps inside, I stand at his threshold. I have not been this close to him in some time. The passage of time has stamped itself deeply into lines on his face.

What I have sensed is truth. His power wanes!

Cardle whirls and satisfaction flickers in my chest when his eyes fill with fear. I can't help it; he looks so comical that a wicked grin breaks past my lips.

"You!" He takes a stumbling step back and his gaze flickers up to check the rune carved over his door.

I say nothing. Let him stew.

"So you have learned a new trick, have you?" he asks, lips twisting in a sneer. "Are you meant to frighten me, because you walk on two legs now, beast? And what will it gain you?"

I glare at him, saying nothing. Unnerved, he darts forward and slams the door closed. My laughter fills the passageway.

To amuse myself, I pace outside his room off and on throughout the night. The chance to torment my warden cannot be missed. Our eternal game has reached a new level. And if I cannot be with Lauren this night, Cardle may have no rest in his comfortable bed. The sooner I can drive him out, the better for me and safer for Lauren.

Cardle and Lauren spend the morning supervising the workmen. They've set up another moving platform for her, so she'll be able to reach me when it's my time.

That afternoon, he stands with her beneath my perch and engages her in discussion. He performs this little show for me, I know.

"I am quite pleased with your efforts so far, Ms. Townsend. I thought we might adjourn to the library to discuss the second contract."

"Th-the second contract?"

"For the replacement statuary. I thought I might offer to let you stay on at the manor to do the work, rather than rent a studio space as we previously discussed. You may convert a room here into a work room. It would save the cost of rental and transportation." He smiles, his attempt at charm apparent.

For the first time, I understand how Cardle must have felt watching another man charm the woman he considered his. Selene was ever a means to an end for him, the terms of a treaty fulfilled. And with shame, I admit she meant even less to me. And she saw me as a way out of her unhappy life, if only for a stolen moment here and there.

Now here is Lauren, on her way to becoming a pawn in the war between myself and Cardle.

"Stay here?" Lauren says, and even from above I sense the conflicted desire in her. To flee from Kinloch and Cardle. To stay at Kinloch with me.

No, Lauren. No.

"Shall we adjourn to the library?"

"I-uh, oh sure, okay." Her hesitation to be alone in the library with him is evident, at least to me.

Cardle smiles again, gracious, inviting.

Sickening.

My Lauren listens to Cardle's proposal, and expresses surprise at his promise to have a contract drafted at his solicitor's office and brought by courier.

"I thought you would wait until the work was complete to make your decision."

"My dear," Cardle leans toward her, then jolts back with an undisguised grimace of confusion. He must sense the talisman in her pocket, but not be able to identify the exact source. "I have seen enough to know you are the one to replace my missing creation."

"*Your* creation?" she asks.

"Oh. Oh yes. I mean to say, my ancestor sketched the original design for that particular piece. I'm claiming undue credit." Cardle has the gall to pretend to modesty by adding, "Though I'm sure your piece will far surpass that which was lost."

"How kind," Lauren says faintly. "I should get back to work."

"Over half the work day is gone. I must insist you take the day off. Perhaps I could give you an overdue tour of the manor." He smile is wide. "You must have supper with me this evening."

"You're staying?"

"At least one more night." He rubs his hands together. "Now, about that tour?"

Lauren has little choice but to acquiesce, or risk raising suspicion.

Cardle brings out every trick he knows to convince Lauren to see him as an affable, landed noble with modern ideas, a man who could charm birds from the trees. Her shoulders begin to relax when her curiosity, as always, gets the better of her. I wish she could hear my warning growl.

Cardle works late into the night, locked in his room and out of my sight. I'm restless without Lauren's company. He cannot leave soon enough to suit me.

"Why did I suspect you would still be out here?" he asks the fifth time he opens his door. "Though I suppose you have nothing better to do."

None of the charm he tried on Lauren presents itself now, only his cold demeanor and haughty attitude.

"Or perhaps you have found something to keep you occupied. Would it be better to say *someone* to keep you occupied?"

My heart threatens to lock up in my chest. I keep my expression disinterested. He can't know about me and Lauren. He can't.

"What is your plan for her, Adriel? To visit her dreams and whisper false prophecies to her until she sees disaster at every turn? Or maybe to convince her that I am a monster and get her to attack me in my sleep? They failed in the past, they will fail again. Maybe you will stand outside her bedroom and let her believe my manor haunted?"

He does not realize Lauren's doorway is unprotected! I almost laugh at his ignorance, and Cook's error.

He clucks his tongue and shakes a sheaf of papers.

"Don't despair, Adriel. I think I have the answer to replacing Selene. Then you'll have some feminine company amongst your kind again."

The papers he's holding catch the light from a nearby sconce. He speaks a word and gold lettering fills the page, the language dead and forgotten centuries ago.

"That little American nobody will design and build her own prison." He laughs, harsh and full of malice. "Once it's done, I'll take possession of the soul she's going to sign over to me."

His lips twist in a triumphant smile.

"Keep your filthy magic away from Lauren," I snarl and lunge toward him. The ward flares to life and I jump back, smothering a cry of pain at the sting of the spell's barbs.

Cardle laughs, the sound of a door swinging on rusty hinges.

"Lauren, is it? How intimate." His tongue darts out, a snake sensing for prey. "So, Adriel has an interest in my future acquisition. Did you give the little bitch the idea to invade my chambers?"

I want nothing more than to rip his throat out, to crush the life from him with my bare hands, to throw him from the ramparts and watch his body shatter on the stones.

To protect Lauren from his machinations.

To avenge myself and the others.

To prevent him from his dark magicks that pervert and twist the purity of our power source to unnatural causes.

"One day," I promise in a deadly whisper. "One day there will be a reckoning, Cardle. And all you have will wither and die."

"You think being free of the stone will mean anything in the long run? You are my prisoner, and you will remain so until I decide to end your suffering once and for all. But I have plenty of time left to me on this earthly plane. As do you." His smile mocks me. "You, and *Lauren*." He spits her name and slams the door in my face.

I should not go to her, not with him here, but I need to reassure myself she has not been harmed.

I scold my beating heart. *Fool. You may have been better off when you were cold and unmoving.*

She's sleeping, and I don't want to wake her, but she must be warned. Cardle will ask her to sign the contract, and I will be trapped in my stone prison, powerless by the sun's light when he does it.

"Lauren," I whisper. She sighs and rolls toward me, but doesn't wake. Bending, I speak low in her ear, warning her of Cardle's plan. "You will remember, and protect yourself."

She murmurs sleepy assent, and I kiss the corner of her mouth before departing.

If Cardle doesn't leave soon, I *will* go mad.

Again.

Lauren

McCardle corners me during my lunch break and presents a simple two-and-a-half page contract and a fountain pen. I take it from him, pinching it between two fingers like it's been fished from the sewer. Nothing about the items scream *danger!* except the sensation of ants crawling up my spine.

"Thanks," I say, the words nearly sticking in my dry throat. "I'll get this back to you."

"I would appreciate it if you would review the paperwork over your meal and return it to me afterward. I will be leaving again shortly."

"Uh."

"Excellent," he says, as if I've said something brilliant. McCardle claps his hands together, and I flinch at the way the sharp sound fills the kitchen like a thunderclap.

I examine the contract carefully, but nothing in the language of it accounts for my unease. The protective spell Adriel gave me grows hot in my back pocket.

Don't sign, blossom. Take nothing he gives you.

My forehead wrinkles in concentration, attempting to catch the wispy tendrils of a faded dream about Adriel.

But the contract appears straightforward, and it will allow me to stay on at Kinloch for an unspecified period of time. To stay with Adriel. Maybe I can find a way to do more to help him, help the others, and still come out of this with my business intact.

The thought of leaving Adriel behind kills my appetite. I leave the contract and go back to work.

McCardle's annoyance comes through when he stands on the rooftop and shouts down to me that I'd left the paperwork unsigned on the kitchen table. I pretend I can't hear him clearly, and shout up that I'll review the contract later and send it to his home in the city.

After a few frustrated minutes, his head disappears from over the side of the wall and I lose myself in the work to shake off the disturbing effect of McCardle's presence.

And the way he kept me from Adriel for two nights.

From the west wall, I miss seeing McCardle zip away in his little midlife-crisis sports car. It's as if the manor itself breathed a sigh of relief on finding him gone.

Adriel paces the rooftop, impatience and barely-suppressed anger evident in the tension of his shoulders. He's discarded the shorts I bought him, but I find I'm used to his naked prowling by now.

I drop my camping mat and satchel on the moss, flinging myself at him. He swings me up into his arms and devours my lips in a hungry kiss.

"Destroy it," he says when we break apart.

"Destroy what?"

"That foul magic you brought here."

He sets me aside and rifles through my satchel. There's no ice cream tonight; we have a lot to discuss and we need focus.

"Ah," he says, and holds up the contract.

"Foul magic is a little extreme. No one likes lawyers but it's just a contract."

The dark look he throws my way begs to differ. He speaks a word, and flicks a finger against the paper.

Under the light of the waning moon, the black lettering fades and golden symbols glow in their place. I reach for the contract, but Adriel holds it out of my reach.

"*Infir,*" he says, and the papers burst into bright green flames.

I flinch back and gawk as the contract burns to ash. A breeze sweeps the ash away into the night.

"He's going to wonder about that," I say, hands on my hips.

"Let him wonder. You must leave here. Tomorrow. Now, even."

"What? No!"

"You are in danger! It is Cardle's plan to trap you in the replacement for Selene. He wants you to willingly sign over your soul, to reduce the chance his darkness will rebound."

I wrap my arms around myself and shiver.

"I won't sign then. But I won't leave, not until I've finished my original contract." The blood drains from my head and I stagger.

Adriel grabs my elbow and keeps me upright.

"My original contract," I whisper. "Is it...do you know? Did I sign..."

"I doubt it, blossom. He does not know what you are." He draws me close and I take refuge in him. "Bring it here to me. Let me examine it inside the Veil."

"I'll bring it tomorrow."

"Tonight. Tomorrow, you leave."

"No."

We argue for the next ten minutes until he's growling in frustration, pulling at his hair and cursing in several languages.

He snarls at me. "You are an infuriating wench."

Infuriating wench! I take a calming breath and remind myself he's from a different time.

But two can play at this game.

"And *you* are a moody thousand-year old lion who better stop using words like wench if he ever wants to get laid again."

When he glowers at me, I can't keep a straight face and end up laughing.

"I am not one thousand years old," he says, petulant, crossing his arms over his chest.

"You forgot moody." I rise on my tiptoes and kiss his cheek. He tries to ignore me, but I lean against him and deliver a trail of kisses along his jaw.

"What is laid?" He's gruff but the fingers of one hand twitch against me, brushing my breast.

"Stop pouting and I'll show you."

In the absence of McCardle, nights are bliss. Adriel stops arguing about my leaving, and our talks focus on how I might free the others.

I deftly avoid discussing how I will free him. To free him means ending him.

"If I freed you from the stone, how come it hasn't worked when I touch the others?"

"You freed me in the Veil. Where I am able to roam about my territory, even if I am still imprisoned."

"So what if I tried it at night, when I'm here with you."

"Your equipment does not exist here."

"But I bring you things from the...from my everyday world. Food. My mat. Maybe I could find a way."

"And when you find they've crumbled away in the Veil, and still exist on the walls by day, as I do, what then?"

He's a frustrating debate opponent.

Some nights we don't speak of it at all, and spend the night talking about anything except the prison of Kinloch Manor.

He's left his mark on me. I've been on my own a long time, not the centuries he's suffered, but a significant portion of my life. Some part of me always hid behind a wall of separation, at parties with casual friends, in classes, even at family reunions. Alone in a crowd, surrounded by people but never part of them.

With Adriel, I finally know what it means to be *with* someone and for them to be part of me. To find the missing piece of myself.

"I should search his room again. I might have missed something."

"No."

"But I—"

"No."

It's the one point he won't budge on, no matter how many ways I approach it. Including bribery with sexual favors.

Stubborn old lion.

"I will search," he says.

"You can't."

"I have a plan."

Adriel's plan sucks.

We have several nights of arguments. Make-up sex is wonderful, but the ongoing battle tarnishes the pleasure of it.

"He'll start back as soon as he can once you destroy the rune. But it will take several hours. You can finish what I task you with and be gone before he arrives."

"But he can refuse to pay me the rest—"

"Lauren," he interrupts. "It is too late for this concern. The man wants to make a trophy of you. He will not care if you have successfully completed your work or not. It will not matter if he provides a good reference, because you will not have a business to return to. You will be trapped here, one way or another. Whether you sculpt a replacement for Selene, or another does, he will steal your life from you."

I don't care anymore about McCardle paying me or destroying my business. I care about what Adriel has asked me to do before I leave for good.

"What if...what if I end up like you? Able to come out at night." My voice shakes. "Able to be together."

He strokes my cheek with the back of one hand. For the first time I can recall, tears form in his eyes.

"It is no life, blossom. Not for you. You belong outside the Veil. And the risk is too great that your magic will not be enough for you to exist here alongside me."

He draws me against him, smothering any further arguments.

"Enough now. Tomorrow night we will act. You will pack and be ready."

Adriel

Tonight I bid farewell to my love for the last time and will see her safely away from the stronghold of my enemy. Lauren's heart will ache upon our separation, but she is ever resilient. She has always been as the delicate primrose that grows in the fields surrounding the manor. A flower that may be stepped on, crushed, but blooms back regardless, always stronger and more plentiful than before.

The plan I recruited Lauren into may fail. And if we fail, I will be doomed to continue on at Kinloch as a man. Alone once more but in my human body, and without Lauren at my side to make the time bearable. To make *living* bearable.

Beg her to change you back to stone flits through my cowardly mind. But no. I cannot ask it of her.

My fallback plan, the one I did not share with Lauren, relies on the resurgence of my deeper magicks. Cardle is in a weakened state, and Lauren has helped me refill the well of my power. Should I be trapped in the Veil beyond this night, I will draw from that fountainhead to engage in battle with my nemesis. Either way, it will all be done soonest.

We expect Cardle to return in a few days, but Lauren will leave Kinloch shortly after sunrise on the morrow, and he will not know until it is too late for him to stop her.

When my thoughts turn solely to Lauren, she slips into the Veil, needing nothing more than my invitation to bring herself into my presence. She stands too far from my reach, the odd shadows thrown by the torchlight hiding the beauty of her eyes from mine. I feel her gaze but it's as if my feet have returned to stone and become too heavy for me to lift so I may cross to her.

She does not move toward me.

Panic pounds through my veins with the force of a hammer striking an anvil. *Will she refuse me on our final night together?*

"Come to me, *fyxe*," I say, but still she regards me from afar.

"You've said that before. What does it mean?" Her voice is a hollow echo across the gulf that separates us.

"It has many meanings. Fire, light, sun, glow, warmth." I count on my fingers. "Heart." The deepest of all uses for *fyxe*. "All meanings depend on how you use it."

Silence falls and creates an unseen barrier. There are many things to speak of before we part, but where to begin? Never has it been so difficult to find words.

"What does it mean the way you use it?" she asks.

How does she not know? "All. You...it...means all."

The spell holding us breaks and we both take one step forward. Lauren's move brings her fully into view and her eyes glisten with unshed tears.

"Come to me, *fyxe*." The words are a caress, but a poor substitute for the real thing. I spread my arms wide and hope.

Lauren

Every time I cross into the Veil, I'm caught off-guard at the sight of Adriel. Most nights, the moment I lay eyes on him, my heart skips before it kicks into high gear and the blood thrums through my veins.

Tonight, however, my blood grows sluggish with the knowledge that this will be the last time we'll be together. The last time we'll talk, touch, stargaze, or sit in silence and listen to the heartbeat of the night.

If I don't move, I can stop time and freeze us in this moment forever. If I do that, I don't have to give him up.

Then he calls to me a second time and the invitation proves irresistible.

He draws me tight against his warmth. The embrace squeezes the air from my lungs, but I don't complain or step away. Instead, I press closer, circling my arms around his waist. We stay entwined with each other until he senses my need for air and loosens his hold.

"I shall miss y—"

"Don't talk," I say, desperate to stop his goodbye. It's a juvenile response, but if it's not spoken, it won't happen, right? *I just want more time*. But one more night together, and I would want another, then another. And then I might never leave Kinloch. "I don't want to talk. Not right now."

"Blossom—" The sorrow in his voice cuts me. To stop the bleeding, I seal my lips to his.

"Don't," I whisper when I break the kiss.

We lock eyes and the ferocity of his expression softens as his pupils dilate. Tension wraps itself around the base of my spine in response to the strange pressure in the air surrounding us. It's the same sensation I'd feel back home before a big thunderstorm rolled in.

The looming storm breaks free and Adriel gathers my hair in his fist. With an oddly gentle tug that contrasts with his tight grip, he forces me to tilt my head back. Something flits across his face, a question almost-asked. I lick my lips and his eyes blaze with sudden heat.

My hands glide down, and I flex my fingers, squeezing the cheeks of his oh-so-firm ass. He releases a soft groan. This is the last weapon in my arsenal to soften his stubborn insistence that I leave Kinloch at sunrise.

"No," he says, picking up on my intentions.

"No?" I ask, and trail one hand up and over his hip before reaching between our bodies and grasping his thickening cock. Anything else he planned to say gets lost to the ether when I give him a firm squeeze.

My mouth curves into a wicked smile and I slowly sink to my knees. His fist remains tangled in my hair, but he doesn't stop me. I squeeze his shaft again, and rub my thumb along his frenulum, causing him to hiss out a sharp breath.

His cock twitches in my hand, waking at a steady pace. I slide my lips over the head. Glancing up at him gives me a glimpse of the raw need that's overshadowed the sadness. Hooded eyes watch me pull back and run the tip of my tongue along the slit. His rod jerks hard in my hand. Before he gets fully erect, I lower my mouth again until the head of his cock bumps the back of my throat and my lips are wrapped around the base.

The low guttural noise that rips from his throat urges me on, and sparks of warmth bloom in my belly. I stop watching him, closing my eyes and savoring the taste of his skin, the tang of his precum, and the swelling of his silken length against my tongue.

Adriel's hand loosens from its fist and grasps the back of my head. The rumble of his pleasure vibrates in the air, and I lift my head, dragging my tongue along the bottom of his shaft from root to tip. I wrap my hand around the base and bob my head up and down, varying the pace until he's growling, barely restraining himself from thrusting his hips in response.

He speaks, but I'm too focused to listen.

Lifting my head, I remind him, "No talking." The threat is clear. Talk, and I'll stop.

He seals his lips shut and tosses his head back, neck muscles straining. I return to teasing him, marveling at how thick and rigid he's become in a few short minutes. I swirl my tongue around the head before locking my lips around it and applying suction.

Adriel lets loose a stream of words in his own language, fists my hair again and drags me to my feet. He crushes his lips to mine, and tears at my clothes like he's reverted to animal form. My tongue clashes with his in a wild dance. I whimper under the onslaught and my legs turn to pudding. He holds my weight easily, one arm tight around my waist, pressing me against his raging erection.

The ripping of my shirt is a faint buzz, barely perceptible over the drumming of my blood pounding in my ears. He yanks my shorts over my hips in one lightning quick move and I kick them away. He sucks my bottom lip, nipping it with his teeth.

I wrap one leg around his waist. His length slides against my wet slit, up, down, smearing us both with our mutual arousal.

"Speak your farewell," he demands, creating a seat for me with his arms and lifting me. I wrap one arm around his neck and both legs around his waist, locking my ankles together.

"No." I grasp his engorged member and line the head of it up with my dripping hole. He holds me tight, refusing to lower me onto his shaft, keeping me from squirming against him.

"I know that you want me," he says, strain in his voice.

I lean forward to kiss him but he avoids my lips.

"Say it."

"No," I reply. I tighten my hold on his cock, and stroke him firmly, once, twice.

"Stubborn wench," he says, panting. He shuffles forward, pressing my back against the cool stone wall. He shifts his hips, adjusts his hold, and drops me onto his straining cock. Adriel thrusts into me with deep, hard strokes, stretching my tight walls.

"More."

The stone scrapes against my back, but I hardly notice in the throes of our frantic coupling. He drives into me, our grunts and cries echoing off the stone walls surrounding us. We've never treated each other with such brutal abandon, and the pain almost exceeds the ecstasy. Tears sting my eyes and I don't bother to distinguish if it's from the intensity of the building pleasure between my thighs, or the ache forming in the center of my being.

The anguish settles in my chest, and I dig my nails into Adriel's back. I'm approaching a precipice and struggle to hold back. Adriel pounds into me, over and over, his eyes clouded with desire and a touch of madness.

"Tell me."

"I'm coming," I cry, instead of the words he demands. With a stunted shout, I convulse around him, my vision whiting out with the implosion.

He buries his face in my neck and with a muted roar, he buries himself deep in my volcanic depths. Adriel's release surges into me, a hot pulse filling me with his essence. His harsh gasps flutter against my skin.

"You will tell me before the night is done," he says, and brushes a lock of hair from my sweaty forehead.

"I'll think about it," I answer, and kiss his lips with a gentle mouth.

The next time he takes me, it's slow and sweet. I whisper the words of goodbye he's been pleading for, and we lie under the stars together one last time.

I destroy the rune over McCardle's door an hour before dawn, and Adriel enters. He trashes McCardle's room and his belongings with the fury of an F-5 tornado. I'm forced to stand in the hallway to avoid being hit with debris.

The search fails to turn up the carved wooden totems McCardle used to entrap the souls he later transferred to the grotesque forms.

"Go now," Adriel says in a rough voice, head turned away from me. We've already had our goodbyes. "Do as I've asked. Dawn comes."

"Adriel, we could still—"

"GO!" he roars, and drives his fist through McCardle's mirror.

I flee to the roof, and as the morning light cracks open the sky, I lower myself down the wall using the movable platform.

Because I've deviated from Adriel's plan.

I smash the snakes surrounding the distorted human face. There's no finesse about my work now; snake heads crumble beneath my rage and debris rains down on the walkway below. Satisfaction lodges in my chest alongside the sharp pain of losing Adriel.

This was one of McCardle's tortured sons, and I take pleasure in wiping the venomous adders from his prison cell. I hope I've freed at least one of the other souls trapped in this place.

Behind schedule, I scramble back to the roof and move to the south wall to use the bosun's chair. I swing my way down to Adriel.

Time to finish what I started yesterday. I raise the mallet and strike it against the pry bar, over and over, venting my sorrow and anger into each blow to Adriel's base.

I'm pouring sweat and trembling with fatigue by the time I free Adriel's form. Now to leverage the grotesque off the perch. My hands slip on the tools. I rub each palm on my coveralls to dry them.

"Goodbye," I whisper, and press a kiss to his cool brow. Salt from sweat, tears, and minerals mingle on my lips, the unyielding stone so unlike the flesh of the man who inhabits this manticore.

Cook stands outside, screaming unintelligible words at me. I shoot her the middle finger and take a swig of water. Physics and the dead weight of Adriel-as-lion work against me. It's all taking too long, longer than Adriel planned. I should have been gone by now.

"I think you better move!" I yell down to Cook, a warble of hysteria in my voice. "Unless you want to be crushed by a pissed off lion with a death wish!"

Stupid plan. I hate this plan.

A grinding sound and movement, at last.

McCardle's car comes roaring up the drive and screeches to a halt in the courtyard. From the corner of my eye, I see him running to join Cook. He sends her inside and takes his turn at yelling.

A suffocating pressure builds in the air around me, and the lilt of McCardle's words sing of turbulent magicks. The charm Adriel crafted for me pulses like a living thing with its own heartbeat where it's tucked inside my bra.

"Can't hear you," I say, panting and straining.

Adriel slides another few inches.

And teeters precariously.

McCardle's words pick up speed, urgent, pushing against me as if they are trying to knock me from the wall.

His hands wave in the air in an intricate dance. The overcast sky grows darker and storm clouds gather over Kinloch. My hair comes loose and whips around my face, briefly blocking my view of McCardle.

Lightning flashes in the sky above me and out of reflex, I let out an involuntary shriek and flinch. Ozone burns in my nostrils. The threat of McCardle's words becomes clear even if I don't know precisely *what* he's saying.

"Go, dammit." I slap a hand against the lion's hindquarters, my hand burning with the sting of flesh against stone. Sweat drips into my eyes, blurring my vision.

The lion springs forward, claws extended, throwing himself into space in a ferocious leap. The weight of the stone, and gravity, should have caused Adriel to crash straight to the ground, but instead he seems to streak like a bullet toward McCardle.

Why is McCardle just standing there? All he has to do is run.

Adriel's words of warning pop into my head. "The wrong movement, a misplaced word, an interruption, they all carry risk."

McCardle can't easily break off his incantation or he risks losing control of the spell he's conjured! A scream rips from my throat, half-triumph, half-fear.

The lion plummets. McCardle's voice turns into a high-pitched shriek, the last sound he makes before the statue flattens him.

I scramble up the side of the manor, take the stairs on shaking legs that threaten to collapse beneath me at any moment and stumble past a screeching Cook, to the front courtyard.

A dusty human form wobbles to his feet.

"No!" I cry out. Sharp dread snakes into my belly.

McCardle can't be alive after that. No magic can keep a man alive after being crushed by a freakin' grotesque falling from that height.

The figure turns toward me and lurches in my direction.

"Blossom?" Adriel asks, shielding his eyes from the harsh light of the sun.

Epilogue – Lauren

"That's really disturbing," I say, circling Cardle, running my gaze up and down, looking for faults.

"You are the one who said we must attend this solicitor's appointment."

"Yeah. I just didn't think you'd actually be able to pull off this shapeshifting thing. It's spooky. You even sound like him."

"I had much time to study his mannerisms," Adriel says dryly, looking at me with Cardle's squinty eyes.

Adriel has been practicing this shapeshifting spell since Cardle met his long-overdue end two months ago. He can finally hold it for several hours at a time.

After Adriel emerged from the rubble of his old form, only Cardle's clothing remained behind. Adriel said centuries of ill-used magic caught up to him in the space of a moment and his body crumbled to nothing.

Cook had followed me outside and fainted dead away when Adriel rose from the dust of her old boss. Adriel wasn't the only one who'd been a lifelong victim of Cardle's magic; once his spells over the manor shattered, Cook's attitude toward the two of us shifted from her usual hostile caution to warm and motherly fussing.

Now that we have his fake identity secured and he can hold the shapeshifting spell, we're going to town to rewrite Cardle's will and leave everything to his new heir, "Cousin" Adriel.

"This plan better work. I'm going to be pretty annoyed if I have to ride to town with you looking like that and it doesn't pay off."

"This is an excellent plan," Adriel says. "Look how well my last plan turned out."

He reaches for me and I dance away.

"No way! You aren't kissing me with Cardle's lips." I open the front door and laugh at him over my shoulder. "See you in the car."

"Adriel?" I call out.

He's standing on the far side of the roof, leaning against the low wall, staring out into the night.

The silvery full moon shines overhead, but the fire pit we installed casts a warm glow over his skin.

I ignore the little pang of disappointment that he's wearing boxer shorts. I had long grown used to his carefree (*naked*) ways in the Veil, but Cook makes a scene when he walks around nude these days.

Had I carved the perfect man for myself, I would never have achieved the beauty I find in Adriel's form. *And he's all mine.* My heart flutters and I'm pulled into his orbit.

"All right?" I ask, slipping my arms around him. I press my ear against his back and place a palm against his heart. The steady beat of it reassures me.

"I am," he says. His large hand captures my free one and lifts it to his lips.

In the three months since he's been free, he hasn't managed to sleep through an entire night. And he can't stand to be indoors for long stretches of time. As a result, we keep strange hours at Kinloch.

"I slept three hours," he says. He turns and draws me into a tight embrace. "I had another nightmare."

His lips brush my temple.

"I wish you had woken me." We've had this discussion several times. "I don't like you to be alone."

"I am not alone, blossom." He tilts my face up so I can see his eyes. "You are always with me, no matter where I am."

"Flatterer." I close my eyes when his lips touch mine. His presence overwhelms my senses and I melt into him.

He delivers a gentle, slow, and thorough kiss.

Endless minutes pass before he lifts his head and says, "Every century was worth it to be here with you now."

Warmth blooms in the center of my chest and spreads. "I love you."

"Back to bed?" The glint in his eyes signal that he's turning his thoughts away from the nightmare that woke him.

"We can stay here." I nod to the pavilion where we've spent most of our nights these past few months.

"No. I must live a normal life again. And I will not mind it if you are beside me." His hands glide down my back and cup my ass. "Or astride me." His lips form a sly smile.

I stroke his cheek. "There's no rush, Adriel."

A flash of disappointment crosses his face and he raises an eyebrow.

"There's no rush to sleep indoors." I correct myself and laugh at the hope that blooms on his face. We both know I've told a partial lie. Cold weather looms around the corner.

But there's time to worry about that later.

"I disagree," he says. A low chuckle follows the declaration.

Adriel lifts me, and I wrap my legs around his waist and throw my arms around his neck. "Take me to our bed then, my grumpy old lion."

"And I will stay the rest of the night," he promises.

"But will you sleep?" I claim his mouth when he opens it to answer. I don't need an answer. We don't plan to waste the night sleeping.

Bonus Epilogue - Adriel

Six Months of Freedom

L auren sleeps curled up against my side, her warm presence a constant reminder that I'm not alone.

I've slept four hours straight tonight, and gone another hour without need for open space driving me to the rooftop.

Lauren worries too much about what she calls my Pee Tee Ess Dee. I tell her not to be concerned. She forgets the secret weapon in the battle to reclaim my life never strays too far from my side.

Her.

When I can't breathe and the walls are closing in, or another nightmare sinks its claws into me, Lauren shines a bright light into my darkness and pulls me out of that trap.

All the motivation I need to conquer my current enemy lies beside me in our bed.

I used to believe my gods had punished me and left me to rot in the Veil. Now I know they tested me, and though I cursed them more nights than not, they rewarded me by putting Lauren into my path.

I check the clock Lauren bought for me and calculate how many hours until dawn. Lauren and I often fall asleep as the rest of the world awakens with the sun.

Now that Cardle is "officially" dead, I am the owner of his ancient clan holdings. Before any other concerns, I must continue cleansing this place of his foul magic. It has sunk into the very soil at Kinloch. Every day we work to pull it out of the ground in the same way one pulls up an invasive plant by the roots so that it cannot continue to overtake the natural order.

Later in the afternoon, I will take Lauren into the nearby clearing to practice her magic. Two months ago, she called a pebble I had buried from beneath the earth. Last week she drew forth a rock the size of my fist, and without breaking a sweat.

"What are you thinking?" Lauren asks, her voice full of sleep.

"I am thinking more of your idea."

"It was just talk. We don't have to do anything yet."

Lauren and I have had many discussions about Kinloch, and about my love-hate relationship with it. The land calls to me, singing with magic and power, drawing me to spend hours walking its peaceful woods.

But the manor chills me to the bone, and even though he's gone, Cardle's presence fills the place. That dark shadow has been nigh impossible to purge.

Lauren has suggested we might sell it.

In return, I suggested she use her talented, magic-wielding hands to reduce it to a pile of rubble. I believe she has it within her to bring down these stone walls if she turns her mind to it.

She nudges me, and throws a leg over my thighs. Neither of us can ever seem to get close enough to the other.

"I want to leave here, my love." I pull the blanket up to her shoulders. "I want to travel with you in the a-ro-plane, and look for what magic might be out there beyond these borders."

"Mmm."

"Your idea of the traveler's inn is a fine one."

"Bed and breakfast," she murmurs, almost asleep again.

"Yes. We will leave it to Cook, and go out into the world. Together." How I would love to explore the wonders she has told me of and those I had once seen on Cook's television, but nothing can tear me from Lauren's side. So if she says we stay, we will stay.

The only thing worse than being trapped at Kinloch Manor for whatever remains of my life? Living it without Lauren.

"Leave." A soft sigh escapes her. "Together." Her breathing deepens and she falls quiet.

For the first time since I have returned to this mortal realm, sleep embraces me.

Acknowledgements & Notes

This book owes a debt to many wonderful writing friends, but especially to my beta readers: Alex Atkins, Galen Gower, Jane Ishly, Leow Jinn Jyh, Rodney D. Lopez, and Avery Other.

I can't forget that this story came about because of a certain delightful little ritual in the 11:59 Writers' Workshop server on Discord. My writing would never have improved enough to give me the confidence to publish a novella if it wasn't for the 11:59ers and their relentless cheerleading. I love you guys and our little corner of the writing weirdos universe.

Thanks also to Pauline Shen and Camsyn Clair for their artwork (and more cheerleading!). Be sure to check out the websites and socials of all the artists who contributed. Their links are on the copyright page.

And a heartfelt thanks to the readers who have picked up this book and read it. I hope you've enjoyed your time with Lauren & Adriel. I look forward to revisiting their world in the future and hope you do as well.

About the author

Mallory Glass is an author who likes to create worlds within worlds for her characters to explore. She writes for those who love to embrace a temporary escape from reality.

She spends her time planning her next big adventure and contemplating the vast cosmos. When she's not writing, Mallory loves stargazing and reading. She lives in the Twin Cities, MN, with her bully of a roommate, fibromyalgia, and a diva pet rabbit.

Her work has appeared in Toad Shade Zine and Humour Me Magazine UK under another name. In October 2025, her short story "Wade vs. Roe" will appear in Dread Mondays, a workplace horror anthology from Whisper House Press. She is at work on Book 2 of Stone & Flame as well as a contemporary college romance.

Find her on Bluesky: @mglaz.bsky.social or on her bare bones website at: https://malloryglass.com/

She loves to hear from her readers.